I0654699

Walter R. Nursey

The Romance of Merry Maiden

Walter R. Nursey

The Romance of Merry Maiden

ISBN/EAN: 9783337347918

Printed in Europe, USA, Canada, Australia, Japan

Cover: Foto ©Andreas Hilbeck / pixelio.de

More available books at **www.hansebooks.com**

The Romance

OF

MERRY
MAIDEN

Or, How the Farm Mortgage Was Lifted by a Jersey Beauty

—

Especially Written for
and Published by . . .

C. I. HOOD & CO., LOWELL, MASS.

1898.

BY WALTER R. NURSEY.

Copyright.

INTRODUCTORY.

The following story as regards its main incidents is founded upon fact.

Fictitious names have in most instances been substituted for the original ones.

The dairy records of the cow, Merry Maiden, and those of the Jersey herd at the World's Columbian Exposition Dairy Tests, with the victory of the Jerseys in open competition against an equal number of Shorthorn and Guernsey cows — the pick of the continent — and the reference to the ultimate and present owner of Merry Maiden, Mr. C. I. Hood, and "Hood Farm" at Lowell, Mass., are historically correct.

The story has been written with a view of showing what can actually be accomplished in the way of releasing a heavily mortgaged farm through the sale of dairy products and by the instrumentality of the most profitable and economical dairy animal in the world—The Jersey Cow.

CONTENTS.

Contents.

The Romance of Merry Maiden

—OR—

HOW THE FARM MORTGAGE WAS LIFTED

CHAPTER I.

Laban Hartland, Merchant.

Laban Hartland, for many years a prominent merchant in a Massachusetts manufacturing town, after a long period of success, came greviously to smash. The causes of his failure were neither remarkable nor original. The blast of a destructive commercial tornado that had swept the land, had so completely thrown him on his knees that, notwithstanding his recuperative abilities and his well known stock of determination, the trade hurricane had left him without a business leg to stand on. His rivals, who by a chain of fortuitous circumstances, and who without any special foresight had weathered the storm, were not slow to imply contributory negligence.

"Laban's obstinate methods," they would say, "and the lack of business acumen," accounted for his disaster. His friends, however, who, by the way, were largely in the majority, declared on the contrary, that "it was a too honest application of the rigid rules of trade on Laban's part, and a

stubborn determination — almost Puritan in its
complexion — which led him to hew to the line. let
the chips fall where they had a mind to, that was
really accountable for his financial downfall."

Be all this as it may, Laban Hartland himself
offered no word of explanation and no word of
complaint. Fortified by his own conscience and
strong in the courage of his convictions, which,
even his enemies admitted, were of too heroic
mold for the exactions of a cut-throat life, he proceeded to gird up his loins and prepared once more
to enter the lists of the bread-winners.

For long years a student of the economic resources of his native land and a blind believer in
the broad principles that the producer of the raw
material must of necessity be an eminently more
respectable individual than the adventurous middle-
man without a stake, or more successful than the
perplexed manufacturer, embarassed with tariff
reforms, he felt that an opportunity had at last
arisen which would permit him to recover direct
from the fruitful lap of mother earth herself, that
peace of mind and comfortable bank account, of
which grasping trusts and tariff-tinkers had at last,
he claimed, succeeded in robbing him.

His failure in business seemed now ready to
offer him in an almost miraculous manner the long
dreamed-of chance to embark in that field of endeavor, which at best, he had hitherto only contemplated from a distance. It gave him, besides, a
reasonable color of excuse to desert the ranks of
trade, without being compelled openly to acknowledge commercial defeat.

With his mind fairly made up in advance, and

the latitude and longitude of the base of his future
operations determined upon, it did not take him
long to decide upon the exact locality where he
would cast his next anchor to windward. With
this same mind thoroughly saturated with the idea
of the omnipotence of cereals in general and wheat
in particular, it is not surprising that the fertile
tracts of north-western Iowa should have readily
attracted and finally arrested him. Its rolling lands,
yellow with the countless tassels of ripening maize,
its terraced uplands that rose in fruitful benches
from the valley of the Missouri, red-gold with the
sweeping fields of grain, so impressed him, as did
also the suave courtesy and disinterested advice of
Colonel Coboss, who had entertained him in his
pilgrimage, that he returned to his Massachusetts
home well nigh intoxicated with the prospect.

"Tell us, father," said Phyllis, as she and her
younger sister, Ruth, listened with keenest interest
to Hartland's glowing eulogy of Iowa's wheat fields,
in his effort to convert them to his new belief, "do
tell us about the horses and the cattle and the cowboys. Wheat fields are, of course, awfully pretty
if there are plenty of blue cornflowers and crimson
poppies mixed up with them, but if you insist on
our becoming rangers, we must have a ranch as
well, you know. Don't you think I'd make a
fetching milk-maid?"

And she put her arms akimbo and gave him a
look that would have melted an anchorite.

"Daddy, dear," said Ruth, "I for one shan't
think of going to — how do you pronounce it, Pop,
Ioway? Iowah? — unless there are cows."

Now the mere mention of cows to Laban Hartland was, so to speak, like the pinning of the flags of all nations on a bull's nose. Of an obstinate disposition and full of crochets, he fostered his pet hobby, "the cultivation of cereals and cereals only, and hang your rotation of crops," to such an extent that the bare suggestion of taxing in any other way, "the possibilities," as he expressed it, "of God's green earth," filled him with resentment.

"Wheat," he retorted, "is good enough for me, and if you girls would only understand that the word farming does not mean muddy byres and crazy cattle that are always wanting to horn you on sight, but that it represents instead, glorious fields of bending grain and huge cornstacks, and bursting granaries, and — and a big bank account, why you had better remain east and stay at school until you learn better, and until you, Miss Ruth, can get over your calf love."

Then, though unconscious of his mild attempt at wit, his temper, which was less than evanescent — even where his motherless girls were concerned — vanished into thin air, and he filliped their pretty ears, a favorite way of his for expressing his affection for the feminine members of his household, and dismissed them.

"I wonder," said Ruth, who, like the bovine objects of her youthful admiration, was of a ruminating nature, "what makes dear old daddy so down on cows and things! He isn't a bit like the original Laban in Genesis, is he, Phyllis?"

"No," said that young lady.

Then after a pause:

"I've been thinking. Bide a wee, dearie, it will all come right in time."

With which somewhat enigmatical reply Ruth had feign to rest content.

The threat of Mr. Hartland to leave his daughters to finish their education in the east was not an idle one. The resolution indeed had been reached after careful consideration, comparatively long ago, and independent of the cow feature it was based on good common sense. A year or so would necessarily have to elapse before he could hope to have his farm equipped and in the perfect running order that his ambition had sketched out. There were buildings to be erected, land to be broken and cultivated, and crops to be harvested and marketed, and which would, he assured himself, of course recoup the outlay for improved machinery and cost of farm stock. While his capital, though modest, was abundantly sufficient to justify him under ordinary circumstances in embarking in such an enterprise, he looked for substantial return from his investment by the close of the second season, at least, when everything would be in good working order, and on a pleasant and permanent footing.

Accustomed to all the comforts and many of the luxuries of the town, he held that it would be an unfair test for his growing daughters to be too suddenly confronted with the daily ordeals of a semi-frontier life; besides, was not their education a matter of far greater moment than learning to estimate the average number of bushels to the acre of standing crop, or the percentage of profit to the producer, on wheat selling at a dollar a bushel in Chicago? These were problems, or rather mere sums in pleasant agricultural arithmetic that would enliven the long winter evenings, when the

girls had finished their "schooling," and were
competent to foot up the credit balances in the
bulky farm ledgers and drive over to the county
bank and make good round weekly deposits on account of the current sales of the farm's product.
With such pictures as these did Laban Hartland
feed his own enthusiasm and essay to soften the
pangs of parting and reconcile his daughters to a
long and trying separation.

" By the expiration of that time," he would say
to himself, "they will be so heartily sick of exile
that a farm devoted exclusively to the cultivation
of Russian thistles even, would be regarded as a
rural paradise, and the absence of cows — the prong-
horned brutes — would never be noticed."

Not that he was in any sense the "stern parent"
with dramatic tendencies; he was generous to a
fault and as sympathetic as a girl is apt to be when
she experiences for the first time the mysterious
workings of the grand passion; and if Ruth had
been earnestly persistent he would have bought
her, for that matter, had she cried for them, all the
two-headed and eight-legged calves in New England, but not as an investment, for he still retained
a sufficient quota of his Scotch inheritance to make
him when combated upon any pet theory, aggravat-
ingly opinionated.

After seeing the girls safely established in a
well known seminary, and under the friendly sur-
veillance of a relative, and having at the last
moment capitulated to the entreaties of his wid-
owed daughter, Mrs. Dorothy Dean, that she and
his little grandchild, Daisy, should accompany him,
Hartland devoted his remaining time and energies

to realizing all that he could in hard cash out of the wreck of his shattered fortune. It is true that the only knowledge he possessed of farming so far had been acquired after a close study of scientific text books and the annual report of agricultural bureaus and societies and through those other indirect sources of information which reach and are retained by any observant man, but this lack of practical knowledge encouraged rather than deterred him.

"I will have no old methods to unlearn," he argued, and as I intend to be a rural plunger and put all my eggs in one basket and confine my attentions strictly to wheat, I must succeed. There is no trick in knowing how to plant wheat. The farmers in Iowa do n't use shot guns, and when the crop is ready to harvest, they tell me out west, the stalks of grain will sing together and call across the prairie for the reaper." And so with this pretty conceit riveted in his mind, the outlook for the future gave Laban Hartland little concern.

A few weeks later, with many blessings and much gratuitous advice from friends and foes, he gathered together the remnants of his household belongings and pulled out of Roxborough. And with a courage and resolution that would have done infinite credit to a far younger man, he boldly turned his face northward, ready, nay, eager, to confront the unknown destiny which awaited him in that remoter land of agricultural possibilities.

CHAPTER II

Colonel Coboss.

Colonel Coboss of Maverick Hall lounged lazily in his sanctum, propelling the blue smoke from a fragrant perfecto with a great show of insistence from a pair of very determined and very closely shaven lips. This smoke cleft the morning air with much the same sort of directness of purpose, as if discharged from the barrel of a Winchester rifle, and was wonderfully indicative of the smoker's existing state of mind. Later it broke out into violet colored waves, as the draught from the open French window caught it, drew it across the piazza and then blew it into the eyes of a troop of brilliant but disgusted butterflies that were fluttering about the morning glories which nodded their dainty heads against the green lattice of the veranda in the faintly stirring air. The shaven lips continued to work more and more energetically, and the puffs of smoke formed into miniature clouds, which mounted to the ceiling and rolled along the fluted cornices, and woke the flies that had overslept themselves, and cleared them out from behind the bookcase and portiere. Some of this cloud of pungent opaqueness swept through the open casement. Outside the butterflies, disconcerted at the rude attack, beat their filmy wings and sought refuge in the rose bushes beyond. The convolvuluses bowed deprecatingly before the assault, checked their coquetry, made scowls of their painted petals, and hid their mortification.

"If," said the Colonel, as he withdrew his perfecto and raised his voice now that the butterflies were out of earshot, and the whisper of the convolvuluses were stilled, "if she is not amenable to gentle measures, we will have to resort to more drastic treatment, by gad!"

The blue lips worked yet more vigorously. The atmosphere grew more opaque. Distorted through the dense drift of swirling tobacco smoke, the speaker's head loomed up like an Alaskan idol. But this was merely an illusion, for the owner of Maverick Hall and its broad acres of very arable fertility was an exceptionally comely man, a faultless piece of human mechanism, strictly symmetrical as to physical proportions, and with an astonishing regularity of feature. A most pleasant type of the transplanted Kentucky gentleman, self contained and affable, with nothing to denote the undercurrent of diablerie which acted as a kind of immoral undertow to a temperament otherwise not entirely destitute of good intentions. This baser side which was under control, to the extent that it was seldom openly manifested and rarely revealed, visibly asserted itself now in a baneful trick of nature, which on just such occasions would steal the abnormal blackness from Colonel Coboss's elliptical eyes, and leave the pupils gray as ashes.

"If Laban Hartland," he continued, raising the pitch of his usually well modulated voice, "does not assert his fatherly prerogative, and the young lady does not respond with due filial promptness. I shall be compelled, however reluctantly," and

the colonel's black eyes grew colorlessly gray, —
" to resort to the — the — well, thumb-screws."

The inquisitorial look which had at first settled
upon the colonel's face here gave way to a broad
smile, as the ludicrousness of the literal thumb-
screw treatment presented itself.

"Ah! bless her," he added, "what, physical
torture? No! no! Why I would not harm her
little finger even, much less her thumbs. Thumbs,
indeed, and thumb-screws! No! that woman's
thumbs are one of her most extraordinary attractions. They are wholly without parallel in my
own experience, and that's not limited. They say,
these palmists and manicure people who profess to
know all about your character from the shape of
your fingers and thumbs, that a thumb that reaches
nearly to the knuckle of the forefinger, with a perceptibly outward curve at the point and a scimitar
shaped tip, invariably accompanies a valiant disposition and a big heart."

Here the Colonel glanced at his own somewhat
unsatisfactory digits, sighed a huge burst of cloud
smoke, drew from an inner pocket a small ivory
tablet and proceeded much after the manner of a
schoolboy trying to draw a pig with his eyes shut,
to sketch very seriously the outlines of an alleged
thumb, based on the above characteristics.

The first attempt allowing the widest play for
the imagination could hardly be regarded as a success. While less like a saw-log than a roll of butter, it might have passed muster for a tolerably
fair roly-poly pudding, spoiled in the cooking.
The incongruity seemed to strike him.

"No! hardly that way," said he, rolling his

cigar between his gleaming teeth until the glowing
point tilted skywards; "thumb, though, is a
deuced hard thing to draw. It's the suspicion of
little wrinkles, and the bit that peeps beyond the
nail that makes it difficult. Whew! that's better."

He now gazed with positive complaisance on an
outline that looked about as much like a bale of
cotton as a girl's thumb. The result, however,
was not entirely satisfactory yet, and he under-
took to elongate the bale and replace the flat iron
bands which bound it with narrower strips until it
looked like the section of a stage brigand's calf en-
veloped in a Greek stocking.

While there is little doubt that the Colonel had
eyes only for the dainty original of his dream away
beyond the burlesque which lay before him, he
still seemed sufficiently alive to the fact that the
thumb as drawn by himself was hardly up to the
standard.

"Ah! ha!" he ejaculated after some minutes
of earnest scrutiny, "I see now what it wants."

Then ensued a further process of elongation and
flattening and some hog-back curvatures, until,
elated with the final success of his endeavor, Colonel Coboss laid the tablet with its staring triumph
of art upon the table beside him.

"Yes," he murmured, "that isn't a half bad
reproduction."

Now if the Colonel's reference had applied to a
certain variety of garden grub, he might have been
reasonably proud of his skill, for at this moment a
big-beaked robin with caterpillar clearly written in
his eye, and a defiant chirp and swoop, dashed from
out the neighboring locust trees, and if the Col-

onel with remarkable intuition, had not divined the bird's natural impulse and hastily concealed the telltale tablets, there is little doubt but that the next instant the robin would have been responsible for a flagrant illustration of the old game of "thumbs down."

"What a cheeky brute," gasped the master of Maverick, as he lit a fresh cigar and made some mental calculation.

"Five semi-annual instalments yet due, and some compound interest. Then there are Scrimp's fees — old brute — they'll have to be included of course to make the whole thing thoroughly judicial and reasonably alarming. Boiled down, I suppose the total will reach at least two thousand five hundred dollars. Now, there arises the crucial question, can he make the payments as they fall due? Unless he lied to me the other day — and even Scrimp admits he don't know how to — they couldn't scare up five hundred dollars among the outfit. Let's see, six hundred and forty acres on the home farm, and six quarter-sections abutting the best grazing lands in the country, farm buildings, furniture, farm implements, crops and every horn and hoof and feather in all Cloverdale. Scrimp was one of the devil's own when he suggested that blanket mortgage and cast iron provision which permits of no second loan without the consent of Colonel Coboss. If the old man had not such extreme views and such punctilious notions as regards honor and financial obligations, he could raise the money without security. Will he do so? No sah!"

In answer to his own interrogatory he lapsed

into the vulgate of old Kentucky, as he was wont
to do when extraordinarily affected, and raised his
voice as if he were pitching the key for a camp-
meeting doxology. Then after a moment's pause
he continued:

"I'll send Hereford over with a note, a confi-
dential letter, to the old boy, telling him that after
our last interview I had decided, upon reflection,
to extend the time and — "

Here the Colonel again paused, for a great
struggle was taking place within his bosom. A
conflict between head and heart; a battle between
the spirit of good and the demon of evil; a contest supported, strange to say, on either side by
the same dominant emotion, the same supreme influence, the same consuming passion — the power of
love. It was not altogether a question as to which
course was the more honorable to pursue, but
rather which of the two would lead to the quicker
realization of his hopes, the consummation of his
desires. For a moment he was honestly anxious
to do what was manly and right, and was about to
yield to that sense of infinite satisfaction which invariably follows upon a conscientious decision.

All the world unfortunately knows, however,
that the most momentous events, even in the
history of nations, to say nothing of those that
determine the fate of individuals, are often wholly
consequent upon some very trifling, and not infre-
quently some absolutely absurd, incident. The
vagary of circumstances was well advertised upon
this occasion. At the precise moment that the
black waves of color were overwhelming the gray
in his handsome eyes, and reason and a proper

sense of everyday human obligation were getting
in their exemplary work, a roistering house-fly,
driven to desperation by a suffocating puff from
the perfecto, lighted for an instant upon the Colonel's shapely nose, and — stung him!

A magnificent moral lay beneath the Colonel's
smarting cuticle, had he but recognized it; not
being constructed upon such philosophic lines,
however, he sprang to his feet with an oath upon
his lips, in place of the discarded Havana, and
pushed the button of an electric bell viciously.

CHAPTER III.

Sarza.

In a few moments the library door opened in response to the Colonel's summons, accompanied by a crisp creaking, as of freshly starched skirts.

"I am here, master," said a singularly soft voice with a purring, half foreign intonation.

"Oh! is that you, Sarza?" asked the Colonel, without turning in his chair, "tell Hereford I wish him to drive over for old Scrimp, right away."

"Mr. Scrimp is here," replied the woman addressed, "or at least, cannot be far away, he has been writing in Hereford's shack all morning."

She drew nearer. The rustling of her skirts — and what a lot these mysterious speaking skirts of women have to answer for — caused unwonted excitement beyond the French windows. The crimson and orange butterflies beat their wings furiously, withdrew from the shadow of the laurels, and, flashing in the sunshine like bits chipped out of rainbows, tumbled over each other in their haste to get closer to the speaker. As for the morning glories, their timidity vanished, each unfolded its striped bodice as if to invite the visitor to the sweet shelter of its bosom. They bowed in unison and nodded a welcome from the trellis, while the leaves of the locust trees and laurels acknowledged with an audible and sympathetic quiver the rustling of the starched skirts.

As Sarza and her influences are closely interwoven with the destinies of the characters intro-

duced into this veracious narrative, it will be as
well to introduce her first as last. Of Louisiana
parentage and creole birth, she had passed the
early years of her womanhood in the service of the
previous generation of Coboss, though not as a
servitor, for on account of her education, largely
acquired by foreign travel, and long contact with
her social superiors, and by reason of her own
native tact, she had, as the foster daughter of the
Colonel's mother, eventually become that lady's
confidante, and the trusted mentor and companion
of himself and sisters, and the faithful repository
of all the Coboss secrets and historic skeletons.
Possessed in a remarkable degree of the peculiar
attributes of her race, she was, it is needless to say,
as loyal in her trust as she was implacable in her
maintenance of what she considered justice. While
seemingly unobservant, and yielding, almost to
the verge of apparent obsequiousness, she was in
reality a woman gifted with the highest perceptive
faculties, and behind her apparent self-surrender,
as inflexible of purpose — when after due delibera-
tion her mind, to use her own language was set —
as were her own starched skirts. Withal she had
a heart as expansive as the surrounding prairie,
and was, it must be added in extenuation of any
inconsistencies which may not seem compatible
with this description, every inch a woman.

Lawyer Scrimp, who worshipped her at a most
respectful distance, hazarded, perhaps, the truest
definition of her character possible, when he spoke
of her to his antique and unwedded sister, as a
"genuine woman, Tabitha, blown in upon the
bottle."

In appearance Sarza was a very remarkable person. Though on the shady side of forty, and a year or so the junior of Colonel Coboss, she did not look a minute over thirty. Her lips were as red, her cheeks as warm and dusky as damask, her teeth as fleckless white, and her coils of abundant hair as black as they were twenty years before, while her figure matured to the limit of permissible plumpness, was physical perfection. She had a "groomed look," as the Colonel was wont to dedeclare, and her comely points reminded him for all the world of one of his own prize Shorthorns. As for her eyes, they were electric jet, and beamed or sparkled or melted in an ever varying and irresistible way, in changeful harmony with the moods of their fair possessor. Scrimp's definition was no figure of speech.

"Mr. Reginald," said Sarza approaching the Colonel, who in answer to her touch had turned to meet a pair of pleading eyes melting with entreaty, "remember your pledge. No," she continued, unheeding his finger raised in remonstrance, "I must speak. Success was never achieved by persecution. I beseech you to be at least just, if not generous, in your treatment of Laban Hartland. Do not be influenced by either Hereford or Scrimp, I know their motives. Resist and desist. Scrimp is but a scheming pettifogger, and poor black Hereford is more madly in —"

"You do me and the other men a great injustice, Sarza," said the Colonel, interrupting and laughing. "I am not planning Hartland's destruction, my dear woman, far from it. I am trying to compass a peaceable conquest all round. Now do please go," persuasively patting her shoulder, "and have lunch prepared and plates set for three."

"Let them try," muttered Sarza as she softly closed the door behind her, and the butterflies retreated and the morning glories drooped. "If it became necessary," and this was said accompanied by a shrug and a contemptuous pout, "I have only to let that old idiot Scrimp touch the hem of my apron even, and he'd be at my beck, soul and body. As to Hereford, poor Jim, ought I tell him all? No, not yet. As for the Colonel and his, well, reckless infatuation, it will bring its own reward. Meanwhile, I fear if he over persecutes Hartland, it may lead to the compromising of Phyllis. I hardly dare look ahead, but if the worst should come, I still hold the trump card!"

"Simple, unsuspecting soul," laughed Colonel Coboss, as the creole's supple form disappeared through the doorway. "If she only knew my real motives. I must have played my cards devilish well; just like a woman, barking up the wrong tree. As for Hereford and Scrimp, they are both mere puppets and will dance to their master's fiddle."

This view of the situation seemed so to impress the Colonel that he slapped the leather riding breeches which encased his shapely nether limbs again and again, and stepped out upon the broad veranda the better to exploit his ideas.

Confronting him, and imperatively arresting his attention, an imposing avenue of swaying sycamores disclosed a vista, the amplitude and pastoral serenity of which it would be impossible to rival in all America. As far as eye could reach leagues of green undulating prairie raced away, and was lost in the throbbing heat of a purple horizon. Islands of timber, of a yet darker green, absolved the rolling sea of grass of all suspicions of monotony, its billowy uplands breaking at the base of an accented sky-line, formed by a barrier of butte-like hills, whose heliotrope colored crests carved faintly serrated patterns on the earth's rim. Munching the juicy tufts of native blue-joint, vast herds of glossy Shorthorns trailed in great spotted bands over the boundless and unfenced meadow, toward a range of lakes that rippled and shimmered in waves of lilac colored heat, magnified in the morning mirage.

"Mine, all mine," said the Colonel airily, while boxing an imaginary compass with a grandiloquent sweep of his hand, "and any woman one would think would be only too proud —" but further soliloquy was abruptly cut short by the sudden announcement of "Mr. Jonas Scrimp, sir, and James Hereford for lunch."

CHAPTER IV

"Cloverdale Farm," Broncho County, Iowa.

"No, Mr. Hartland, sir, it's no use shuttin' one's eyes to facts, when they are as plain as the brand on Black Hereford's stallion. Rain or no rain, it's all one, and we'll never so much as thresh ten thousand bushel of wheat this season. Last year times were, well, bad enough, the Lord knows, but this year we couldn't have it much worse than it is, I guess, even if the devil himself was runnin' the shootin' match."

The speaker was Joe Parilla, overseer and stable-boss on the Cloverdale Farm, and as he uttered his alarming ultimatums, he continued vigorously to pull straws from a loaded wagon, against a wheel of which he leaned, and with a sharp knife whittled the stalks into innumerable slender toothpicks.

"Well, but, Joe, assuming that the upland crop is, as you say, all scorched, and proves an utter failure, the six hundred acres on the river bottom will surely yield an average return."

"An average yield of sapless fodder, yes sir, but we have no stock to feed it to, and we ain't achin' for litter. We can plough it in as a fertilizer of course," and he snickered and looked up from under his half-closed lids, "or," he added, "you can sell it for ensilage perhaps to the Co-

boss crowd for their money-making Shorthorns.
See here, Mr. Hartland," he continued, "that
crop down there alongside the creek'll never head
out. You can bet your sweet life on that, and no
disrespect intended. You sowed that bottom land
too late. We are not raising Jonah's gourd's.
Now, not bein' a married a man," and he pulled
up the slack of an overall, rested one foot on the
hub and looked a little sheepish, "my opinion
perhaps should n't cut any great figure, but I do
know that babies are babies, and wheat is wheat,
and I don't reckon that you or any other man.
beggin' your pardon, should any more expect to
raise wheat in two months, than you could expect
to raise a family irn twelve. We've no string on
Nature, sir; Nature hoes its own row."

"Exactly, Joe, exactly," said Laban Hartland,
repressing a smile, and resisting the temptation to
continue the parallel, "but you see," and he
spoke almost deprecatingly, "it is not altogether a
matter of time alone, other conditions have to be
considered both in the case of wheat as well as in
that of, I think you said babies. though I hardly
think your argument a sound one. I relied, you
see Joe, and not without some show of reason,
on the 'other conditions'."

"Don't you think, Mr. Hartland," then insisted the unabashed Joe, "that the 'other conditions' right now are favorable for shuttin' partly
down on wheat and tryin' a rotation of crops.
You might also pick up a few head of stock to
eat, say the garden truck, and a good milch cow
or two —"

But Joe got no further, for with a shrug and a

snort the Laird of Cloverdale turned on his heel
and disappeared in the adjoining shrubbery.

*   *   *   *   *   *

Four summer seasons have passed over Laban
Hartland's head since we left him at Roxborough,
preparing for his exodus into the promised land.
Four seasons, sad to relate, loaded down with a
record of inexperience, misdirected effort and un-
preventable climatic drawbacks, which latter an
adjoining and like-suffering farmer attributed, not
in his own, but Hartland's, case, to a well-merited
visitation of God.

" Ef it hadn't bin fur ole man Hartland's pig-
headedness," he complained, " in seedin' down his
hull farm with wheat four gol-durned seasins runnin' and defyin' all the laws o' rotatin' and tillin',
thar wudn't ha' bin no need for the fule rain-
maker, and none on em' wudn't ha' bin in th'
soup."

On reaching his destination in the valley of the
Missouri, Hartland had at once with his usual in-
domitable energy set about making the necessary
preparations for converting into one huge wheat
field a portion of unbroken prairie, which he had
purchased from Colonel Coboss on time.   This
with characteristic hustling, and after considerable
outlay in cold cash, he succeeded in accomplishing
in very short order.

Substantial farm buildings were erected to
shelter the working stock he had also bought
from " my friend the Colonel," at metropolitan
prices. Expensive gang-plows and the " latest
thing out" in harvesters were also secured at
alleged cut rates from the insinuating agent at

Broncho City, the county town. Two barns, with innumerable patent attachments for unloading wagons and equipped with automatic doors and self-acting roofs, were also regarded as indispensable, while two or more windmills with no apparent mission in life other than to whoop it up perpetually, cast their shadows across the home paddock, exchange their whirring confidences, and knew infinitely better than did their unsuspecting owner which way the trade winds blew in that section of Iowa.

A granary sufficiently spacious to hold the season's product of twenty-five bushels to the acre, was also constructed, its hungry maw never destined to be filled. And when these were all complete, a charming wooden dwelling, a compromise between an Indian bungalow and an old Colonial manor-house, with a broad piazza and gleaming with white paint, was raised upon the green banks of the Osage river, amid the rustling shelter of a grove of sycamore. Everything, in fact, that his uncontrolled fancy could suggest, and the limited capital at his command could procure, for the better handling of the bountiful product of the fecund prairie, was enlisted. Indeed, nothing that the most exacting farmer could desire was now wanting save the coming harvest. Yes, the "harvest:" and it seemed to the ex-merchant of Roxborough that the word so little considered heretofore, the farmer's imperial tribute to the nation, now came to him with an entirely new and most significant interpretation.

It must not be supposed from this story of Hartland's expenditures that he was either a spendthrift, in the broader acceptation of the term, or an utter simpleton as regarded money matters. Accustomed to dealing in large transactions, and completely impregnated with the belief that wheat was paramount, he was yet fully alive to the fact that he was speculating in futures. When cautioned on this point by his friends, "Tell me," he would retort, "if you can, of any one branch of industry, the trade pursuit of which is free from gambling? 'T is merely a matter of degree."

He was so completely possessed with the idea that at least ordinary success must follow his enterprise, that side issues gave him no concern whatever. "The Dalrymples and the Grandins in Dakota raised tens of thousands of acres of wheat successfully," he said, "and why should n't I have my bonanza farm, though on a smaller scale?"

The mere fact of an extra hundred dollars or so spent on farm machinery, was as nothing, he maintained, compared with the ultimate indirect profit derivable from the services of a superior implement. The mortgage given to Colonel Coboss in part payment of the land and farm stock, though it was of the "blanket" order, and if it did include, through Jonas Scrimp's ingenuity, everything, "lock, stock and barrel" in all Cloverdale, why it was "western style," and after all, not such a piece of sharp practice as it might at first sight appear. What with the unexpended balance of his capital on hand, and the proceeds of sales of farm produce, the payments could easily be met. As for running expenses, well, without giving the matter very close attention, he estimated he would still have

plenty, for, from the standpoint of a farmer, he
always understood in a vague way that it was true
that the farm would be "self-sustaining, you know,
from the start." He dismissed this feature of the
situation with glittering generalities, but neglected
to invest in either pigs or poultry, and actually
bought his daily supply of milk from Cornelius
Kobb, his sorely perplexed brother granger, a
portion of whose smaller holding abutted on his
own.

His enthusiasm, too, and confidence in his own
enterprise, was no less astonishing than strangely
infectious. From at first being regarded as a "dead
sure mark," upon whom it would be easy to unload
unsalable articles, his methods in which he was
so sincere a believer, were so unflaggingly followed by him, that the creed of this new apostle
of farm culture, while it was regarded with suspicion by the many, was actually imitated by the few.

All his efforts, however, for the first season,
proved as might have been expected, stale and
unprofitable. Instead of starting in and preparing
the ground for the seed in the first place, bright
and early, he wasted valuable time in erecting the
farm premises, all of which, as pointed out to him
by Jack Hardisty, chief ranger on Dr. St. Lambert's neighboring ranch, and for whom he had
conceived a very strong regard, might far better
have been postponed until the fall. There was, of
course, no crop, but the harvest for the ensuing
year, he explained to Hardisty, owing to the magnificent condition of the soil, which had been har-
rowed until it was sore, would more than make
up for the apology of a crop, which, had the ground

been seeded, under the circumstances, would have amounted practically to nothing.   He would give mother earth a rest, now that she knew what was expected of her, so that she would be in perfect condition for her next season's great effort of maternity.

CHAPTER V

Laban Hartland, Wheat King?

The following season, as every farmer in the entire northwestern states remembers to his cost, was one of disastrous climatic surprises. A deluge, a frost, and a drouth, in unfair succession, swept the country in wayward waves. While Cornelius Kobb's six hundred and forty acres of mixed farming lands were rendered only partially unproductive and Colonel Coboss's thousands of acres of grazing ground still offered reasonable sustenance to his flocks and herds, Laban Hartland's one thousand acres in wheat, with local partiality and unfair discrimination, received the full brunt of the attack. The standing crop on about one-third of the acreage was ruined. less than one-third actually yielded an average. while the remainder only harvested about eight bushels to the acre.

In the empty bins of the great granary that was constructed to hold one hundred thousand bushels, if need be, the grains comprising less than eight thousand bushels of wheat shouted to each other as best they could, over hollow sounding partitions, the pathetic story of their survival.

"The odds are against me, this time," was the only comment Hartland was known to make.

No word of complaint passed his lips. If discouraged, he was certainly not cast down, for he applied himself with undiminished — if it did appear to Mrs. Dean somewhat pitiful — zeal to the preparations for another season. At sixty cents a bushel, however, his wheat paid little more than half the expense of cultivating even the productive acreage, to say nothing of that of the three hundred acres ruined by the elements. The remainder of the expense account had to be met out of his diminishing capital. The interest on the investment and the payments on the account of Col. Coboss's mortgage, also taxed heavily his bank balance, while the farm failing to be "self-sustaining from the start, you know," and not being equipped with kitchen garden, cows, pigs or poultry, contributed nothing towards the support of the establishment, all of which had to be borne by the "nest egg."

A rehearsal of the reverses of an honest man is never very pleasant reading, but as this story has the two-fold purpose of recounting truths and pointing a practical moral, the necessity for the publishing of the bald, uncompromising facts will become apparent.

Another winter came and went, and Hartland had improved the opportunity, to his own satisfaction, at least, in devoting the long evenings to the further theoretical study of what had now become almost a monomania with him — the study of wheat. His bookshelves groaned with works on the cultivation of cereals. Those on wheat, however, were the only ones that bore the earmarks of reference. His table was littered with memoranda and calculations, and a report of the proceedings of some agricultural society or other might always be seen peeping from his pocket. Indeed, at his own suggestion, he had read a paper on

"The Future Wheat Possibilities of Iowa," before the members of the Broncho County Development Association, which was, however, coldly received, the majority of his audience being either corn raisers or stockmen.

"If you could only persuade your father to devote half of the energy he wastes on wheat," said Dr. St. Lambert, the proprietor of the great Cushla Ranch, of which Hardisty was chief cow boy, addressing Mrs. Dorothy Dean, "to the raising of cattle, or to the pursuit of mixed farming, he'd coin money hand over fist."

"O, Doctor!" she said, "that does not come within the range of even my wildest hopes. Phyllis is the only one who has the slightest influence with him, and as neither she nor Ruth will be here for a year yet, not until next spring, I am in despair."

In regard to the return of the girls, however, Mrs. Dean not being entirely in the confidence of her father—indeed, who was?—she was altogether astray in her calculations.

A sudden determination had possessed Hartland to anticipate by nearly a twelve month, the order of his plans, as originally mapped out. To begin with, he was devotedly attached to his daughters, and while not admitting it, was peculiarly susceptible to the influence of Phyllis, who was gifted with an extraordinary share of personal magnetism, and an unusual degree of what Joe Parilla was pleased to designate as "horse sense." He was hungry to see them again if only to "fillip their ears," and listen to the music of their chatter. Further than this he was so confident that the then ensuing season was going to be one of magnificent agricultural conquests, that he wanted them to share with himself the pleasure of watching the gradual development of his gigantic field of wheat, fifteen hundred acres in all, and upon the final and perfect fructification of which and complete vindication of his theory, he had not only staked his reputation, but many a crisp bank note as well. Hence April of the current year found Phyllis and Ruth full of expectancy, and bewildered with the novelty of their new western surroundings, permanently domiciled in the white bungalow on the banks of the Osage river.

*   *   *   *   *   *   *

It was now July and it was with no small degree of mortification and growing resentment that Laban Hartland turned his back on Joe Parilla and that worthy's advice, and in full view of his parched wheat fields, which a break in the thicket disclosed, halted alongside a big cotton-wood, and for the first time began to question the value of his theory of placing all his industrial eggs in the one basket.

However encouraging it might appear in the abstract, there seemed to be a fallacy about the principle when applied to the exclusive cultivation of wheat. Even the cherished superstition in regard to odd numbers had deserted him. Here was the third season, and if Joe Parilla's prediction was to be verified — and in the face of events, who could doubt it—why, what was to become of them all? This state of affairs could not last forever. Money going out all the time, and expenses far away in excess of the promised receipts. With the next instalment on Coboss's mortgage to be paid, and the notes on the farm implements to be taken up, and both of these were imperative, what would there be left in the bank to carry on future operations, and perfect his further scheme of converting the remainder of the two thousand five hundred acres into one vast field of waving golden grain?

Raising his head at this juncture, Hartland's eyes again rested on hundreds of acres of sickly yellow stalks of sere and stunted wheat. Another season of unprecedented drouth, supplemented largely by his willful obstinacy in neglecting the advice of his friends to sow earlier, had served to fill the cup of his disappointment to the very brim. Across the western rim of the horizon a sinking blood-red sun was discharging its last baptism of blistering, remorseless rays. They smote without pity the bowed and thirsty heads of grain, whose creaking stems swayed and rattled in vain lament under the influence of faint puffs of wind which stole from the valley, and woke them into compulsory acts of homage.

A tide of conflicting emotions stirred the inmost recesses of Hartland's tortured heart. Was this the "magnificent agricultural conquest" that he had promised his daughters? Was this the crowning spectacle of triumph that he had hurried them from peaceful Massachusetts to share? What must they think of him? To what kind of home had he brought them? A moment more, and, carried away with the realistic sense of his misfortune, he was dangerously near a physical collapse.

At that moment, however, like the clarion tones

of a silver bell, a voice reached him through the whispering tree tops and above the querulous murmur of the sea of wheat. It revived him like a glass of sparkling water. What was it? Listen! It reaches him again. Now it is nearer, and yet nearer still, and now with a perfect flood of melody, the rich notes of a full contralto burst their way through the broad-leaved lindens, possessing trembling wheat field and somber thicket, and fall upon Laban's sore heart like heavenly dew:

"Home, home, sweet, sweet home!
Be it ever so humble, there's no place like home.
'Mid pleasures and palaces, wherever I roam
Be it ever so humble, there's . . . . . ."

A tall gracious figure, dressed in a dark green riding habit and swinging a broad grey sombrero emerged from the wooded pathway.

The song was checked.

"Why, Daddy!"

The next moment Phyllis Hartland was in her father's arms.

CHAPTER VI

A Council of War.

"Ah! Good morning, Scrimp; morning, Hereford," said the master of Maverick, as in answer to Sarza's announcement he re-entered his study and greeted these two worthies.

"Your humble servant, sir," squeaked the individual first addressed, a small stoop-shouldered, "red-complected," wizened kind of man, with that quality of voice generally attributed to a chicken with the pip. Hopelessly diminutive under the most favorable conditions, Scrimp's bowlegged charms were at the present moment subjected to an unusually severe test, as standing between two magnificent giants, he turned his pale, underdone little face upwards, and challenged with his watery eyes from behind the merciful cover of his green goggles, those of Coboss, black and unfathomable as night.

"Friend Jonas has been at my shack nearly all morning, Colonel," broke in James Hereford, "we've been trying to shake the tangles out of that St. Lambert deal. I was on the Cushla range yesterday, and saw the doctor, and had a dead cinch on the contract, when who should ride up and cut in but that wolf, Jack Hardisty."

"Well," said the Colonel, leading the way to the dining room, "did he eat you?"

"Hardly, but he wanted me to eat my own words."

"Hope it hasn't taken away your appetite.
Will you have a bit of undercut?" And the Colonel, with the skill of a veteran, carved a delicious
slice from the cold sirloin roast before him, and
passed it to Hereford.

"Thanks. If I could have given him an
'upper cut' I would have been better pleased,
though."

Hereford was a singularly handsome man, of
the sunburned, olive type, and bore a striking re-
semblance to Colonel Coboss, a likeness that
seemed more than accidental. Twenty-three years
the junior of the master of Maverick, the latter
carried his middle weight of years with such care-
less unconcern, that the alleged discrepancy in age,
if a fact, was but little apparent. The two men
would have passed anywhere for brothers. In
Hereford's case, however, while fortunately he
was not afflicted with the detestable trick of
nature, that at times marred the black beauty of
the Colonel's eyes, there was an ever present cruel
line that lurked about lip and nostril when his
features were in repose — a sort of devil's birth-
mark. This was instantly dissipated if he smiled,
when his expression, to borrow from Mrs. Dean's
vocabulary, became "seraphic." His reputation,
however, with or without just cause, if popularity
was a true test, was none of the best. Among
the men on the ranches his record for truthfulness
had been impeached. The every day, all-round,
picturesque liar was a type, of course, both encouraged and forgiven; the man who forfeited
his word of honor — never. Other peccadilloes
were attributed to him, which, if not actually dis-

creditable, did not serve to raise him in the estimation of his cowboy partners. They drew the
line between being "full of the devil" and "full
of deviltry." Whispers of these very shortcomings and his unvarying courtesy to the opposite
sex in his own social rank, actually enlisted — im-
perceptibly to themselves — the sympathy of many
a good woman on his behalf.

"Black Hereford," they were wont to declare
with a good deal of perhaps pardonable and certainly very pretty emphasis, "was as much sinned
against as sinning." This declaration of faith
which could hardly be called an original mode of
expression even in Broncho County, seemed, however, to ease them.

On the list of his very ardent admirers was
Miss Tabitha Scrimp, a contemporary counterpart of her bandy-legged brother, Jonas. If the
gossip of the cattle-runs could be relied upon, she
had frequently and openly expressed herself as
quite ready to sacrifice her feelings, condone all
Hereford's shortcomings, and take him, peccadilloes, chapperajoes, sombrero and all, to the doubtful shelter of her trembling, if somewhat withered,
bosom. So far she had not been called upon to
make the sacrifice.

*　　*　　*　　*　　*　　*

"That's a matter," said the Colonel, referring to
the Cushla tangle, "that you and Scrimp and the
doctor must fight out among yourselves. Don't
drag me into it. By the by, Scrimp, what's this
agitation they're getting up in town over these
new-fangled importations of St. Lambert's?"

"Well, sir," said the little red-headed attorney,

balancing a large dill pickle on his fork, and regarding it with as great a show of gluttony as he would a professional fee, "the town has just gone mad over these Guernsey and Jersey cows, which the doctor, it seems, brought with him last fall from the east."

"I know all about that, my good man. What I asked was what's the nature of the agitation, d'ye understand?"

Scrimp's reply was unintelligible; he was struggling with the dill pickle.

"Well, St. Lambert, you see," said Hereford, coming to the rescue, "has been to a lot of expense, and I expect he wants to unload some of his new stock. There's no doubt that he's got some beautiful cows, but whether they are anything like what he cracks them up to be is a critter of another color."

"You are right to a certain extent," interrupted Scrimp, who had now conquered the pickle and was preparing to attack another, "but the doctor is not so anxious to unload as you imagine. In fact, 'Jersey Jack' told me none of the outfit were on the market. It seems that St. Lambert is aching for an opportunity to obtain an expression of opinion from all the stock experts and ranchmen in the county. While you were away last winter, Colonel, the dairy qualities of Shorthorns, Jerseys and Guernseys were, without intending a joke, the stock theme of conversation at every camp fire. Then from the ranch and farm house, the topic drifted downwards, until today, I venture to say, there is hardly an able bodied man or woman in Broncho County, who has not an opinion one way or another on the subject. Why, my respected sister, Miss Tabitha—"

"Excuse the interruption," said the Colonel, "but how is Miss Scrimp?"

"Finely, Colonel, finely, thank you; as well as can be expected; that is, as well as usual. A touch of the meagrins," and he looked over the top of his green goggles at Hereford, expecting an expression of sympathy, but disappointed in this, continued with a pickle obstructed sigh, "she leads a lonely life, sir!"

"You were saying," said the Colonel.

"Yes, I was saying," resumed Scrimp, "that my sister tells me that our girl, our hired help, who is very friendly with a man called 'Dago Phil, the Rustler,' you know him, has been quite busy lately making 'buttons' for one of the stores in town. She's remarkably clever with her needle. These buttons, which have an 'S' or a 'G' or a 'J' worked on them, as the case may be, are now actually being worn by the members of the contending factions of cattle enthusiasts."

"I do n't understand," said Coboss.

"O! Come now, Colonel, do you mean to tell us you do n't catch on?"

"Listen," said Hereford, "here is the interpretation," and he pulled a copy of the Broncho County Rustler out of his pocket and read as follows:

"'The interest of the cattlemen in the moot question of bovine superiority remains unabated. Not only have a lot of "buttons" been worked off on the excitable cowboys, especially on the Cushla and Maverick ranches, but our respected fellow cit-

izens have caught the milk fever also; and now to
clap the climax the small boy has chipped in and is
raising the echoes of our street corners with the
following inspiring refrain:

> "'S stands for Shorthorns, with coats soft as silk;
> G stands for Guernseys, who give us good milk;
> But J stands for Jerseys, as fair as a dream,
> Who beat all the records for butter and cream.'"

"What ineffable balderdash," shouted the Colonel, "and what infernal lies. It's just the sort
of milk and water twaddle I suppose one might
expect in the poet's corner of a hayseed sheet."

"Seriously, though," said Scrimp, who was
actually trembling over Coboss's sudden outburst,
"the Cattle Breeders Improvement Association, I
am told, have taken the matter up, and are going
to call an open meeting at the town hall to discuss
the respective merits of the different breeds. I
heard your name, Colonel, mentioned as the one
most likely to be coupled with the advocacy of the
Shorthorns."

"Indeed, 'good wine needs no bush,' Scrimp.
It would be too much like begging the question, it
seems to me. The deuce take the impudence of
these Channel Island cowmen. My word for it,
Mr. Jonas Scrimp, the Shorthorn is the greatest
dairy animal in the world. St. Lambert must be
crazy."

"St. Lambert is a convert to Guernseys," said
Hereford, "it is Jack Hardisty who is the cham-
pion of the Jerseys. It is a pity he does n't make
a proselyte of old Hartland."

"It's about time some one converted the old
sinner from the error of his ways," added the

Colonel, " he is going to agricultural smash head-
long. 'Wheat is king, rotation of crops be hanged'
is the only motto he pins upon the wall."

"Yes, his faith in wheat is remarkable," said
Hereford. "It's a passion and would be magnificent if it was n't so pitiful. He won't raise as
much to the acre as he did last year even, and with
wheat at forty cents, it won't pay a third of his
working expenses."

"How much has he under crop?"

"Fifteen hundred acres, his man Parilla told
me. Five hundred acres of it will never be harvested. It was sown too late, to begin with, and
the drouth killed most of that which was seeded
earlier. If he thrashes ten thousand bushels it
will surprise me."

"I made him an offer some weeks ago for half
of his standing wheat stalks for fodder. Three
dollars an acre."

"Did he accept?" asked Scrimp.

"No, he laughed at me. You know his way,
an irresistible way. It is impossible to get angry
with the man. What a great promoter he'd make;
he had me almost convinced, though I knew to the
contrary. 'Colonel,' he said, 'there' pointing in a
certain direction, 'are a thousand acres of wheat
maturing slowly, but none the less surely. I shall
raise from eighteen to twenty thousand bushels on
that bit of land alone. With wheat at sixty cents
it will enable me to pay all my year's expenses and
take up the mortgage you hold on Cloverdale.
Which shall I do? Make twelve thousand dollars
out of the grain or get four thousand seven hundred for the stalks — if you bought the whole crop

even — and then go four thousand three hundred dollars in debt for working expenses? Besides which, you would still hold the mortgage. I am sure you'll excuse me,' he added, with a chuckle, 'but I guess I'll thrash it out. Cloverdale is destined to be the bread basket of the Osage valley'."

"Two good seasons running would set him on his feet," said Scrimp.

"Not even if he raised twenty-five bushels to the acre with wheat at present prices," said Hereford.

"His only hope of salvation," said the Colonel, "rests in stock or corn, or, failing that; mixed farming. What's the balance of the mortgage, Scrimp?"

"Twenty-five hundred dollars," replied the attorney, "plus the interest and legal expenses."

"When's the next payment due?"

"Five hundred dollars in September."

"Will he be able to come up to the scratch?" asked the Colonel.

"It's very doubtful."

"Don't know about that," interjected Hereford, "young Dolla, the broker, told me he knew for a fact that the old man had at least two thousand left to his credit."

"Even so," said the Colonel, "look at his expenses."

"Be that as it may, Mr. Hereford," said Scrimp, "I do know this, for our hired girl, Lena, told my sister, and Tabitha — Miss Tabitha" — Jonas had been instructed by his sister invariably to prelude any mention of herself by the sweet prefix denoting her untrammelled rank in the sisterhood —

" Miss Tabitha told me that both the Hartland girls had been making money out of ' buttons,' and that the elder one was giving Lena music lessons, and she such a haughty jade that —"

The sentence was never finished.

" How dare you, sir," said the Colonel and Hereford at one and the same moment, and simultaneously springing to their feet. " Miss Phyllis—"

But this sentence, in duplicate as it was, was also destined never to be finished. for at the same instant that the two visibly excited men rose from their seats and stood towering above the shrinking frame of the petty attorney, both moved by one common impulse to the same trick of action and similarity of speech, the parlor door was suddenly flung open, as if the name of " Phyllis " was as potent as the wand of a magician, and Sarza stepped into the room, bearing a tray with a decanter of Bourbon whiskey and a box of perfectos.

The situation, which at first threatened an almost tragic denouement, now hovered on the ragged edge of comedy.

Scrimp, no longer shaking in his boots, was cultivating an attitude and a look of unutterable things, for Sarza's benefit, but his blandishments were entirely wasted. The ludicrous points of the little man, however, were brought into more ludicrous prominence than ever, while Colonel Coboss and Hereford, after one swift, mutually inquisitorial glance into each other's eyes, awkwardly endeavored to resume their seats and recover their self-possession.

A trying pause of a few moments' duration. was broken by Coboss, who, turning to the lawyer curtly instructed him to "prepare at once a statement of Hartland's indebtedness, with a view of enforcing any proceedings necessary," and, lighting a cigar, left the room.

Hereford sought the piazza, and Scrimp, with unusual celerity, the hall, for his hat and overcoat, where he was intercepted by Sarza, who, placing her finger upon her lips, conducted the astonished notary into her own apartments.

CHAPTER VII

Phyllis.

" Why, Daddy ! "

To Phyllis Hartland the sudden coming upon her father was a surprise, as pleasurable it was as unanticipated. It is true she was searching for him, but the " Linden Lane," as the girls had christened the pathway through the bluff. was the least likely place in all Cloverdale where she might reasonably have expected to find him. It was little used save by her sister and herself, leading practically to nowhere in particular, losing itself, indeed, in its own circumlocution, as it threaded its aimless way by the gray white bolls of cotton-wood and maple, or under the shade of a fragrant red cedar, that would stand out in marked contrast against the lighter green of the lindens.

" Why, daddy, dear," she repeated, enunciating the familiar title, time worn as the everlasting hills, but with a full, rich velvety intonation that gave it a new significance, while she gently took her father's hand and led him unresistingly to the prostrate trunk of an old moss grown tree.

She stood before him absolutely unconscious of her artistic pose, her uncovered head crowned with the ample coils of her own bronze brown hair. The rounded outlines of her person liberally though modestly revealed by the closely fitting habit, now bathed in the afterglow of the sunset, made her appear to Hartland more like a figure escaped from the stained window of some ancient cathedral, than one of his own flesh and blood—a glorious type of the most perfect maidenhood.

" Why, Phyllis, my dear child! "

This was the extent of Laban Hartland's salutation. None of the usual assertive buoyancy; a rising in the throat; a sudden access, not of physical pain so much as of an inexplicable sensation of weakness; a mortifying surrender of the strong will, an uncontrollable desire to cast himself on the fallen leaves and weep his life away. Ah! but he would fight it down, while she, with maternal instinct, inherent, if not self-understood, even in the youngest of her sex, though divining the emotion that possessed him, abstained from too great display of open sympathy, but, guided by the love that stirred her heart, and with rare feminine tact, restored to him, ere he knew his condition was discovered, his lost power of control.

" Now, isn't this just too delightful for anything," said Phyllis, seating herself beside her father and throwing the fawn colored sombrero with its hawk's wings at her feet, where it formed, perhaps not altogether accidentally, a striking contrast with the dark green folds of her skirt.

" Give an account of yourself, miss," said Laban.

" Well, I rode over to Maverick Hall to lunch and to have a chat with Sarza; we always find so much to talk about, father. What a dear, good woman she is! Then, I went into town to give — at least to do a little shopping, and when I came home I found the bungalow deserted. Roxey,

with her eyes very wide open if you please, told
me Dorothy, Ruth and Daisy had driven over with
Dr. St. Lambert to Cushla Ranch. Do you know
I actually think that the doctor is gone on Ruth.
Then, as I was dying to see you, I took Starlight
to the stable to Joe Parilla, who said he was sure
you were not far away, and then I followed Linden
lane, not the least because I expected to find you
here, but because I wanted to get cool first. There!
isn't that a long story? I am almost out of breath."

She turned to Hartland suddenly and kissed
him.

"Dear father," she whispered, with a long
drawn out inflection on the adjective, as she placed
her hand on his.

"Bless you, Phyllis," he answered returning
the pressure, "you are indeed my ministering
angel."

And they both knew the unexpressed emotion
of each other's heart.

"And what did you buy in town, pray?"

"This," she said springing to her feet. "What
do you think of it, dad?" and she placed the sombrero jauntily on her great coils of dark chestnut
hair and stepped back to confront him.

What did he think of it? Had he been any one
but her father, he would have taken her in his
arms then and there, and considered death a light
punishment for the offense. Even as it was, Hartland was stirred into a sudden recognition of his
daughter's great beauty, and the magnetic influence
of her personality. It came upon him like a revelation. Behind her figure, as she stood facing him,
a small clearing in the bush presented in the dis-

tance an uninterrupted view of endless undulating wheat-fields, which lost themselves in an amber horizon. Framing this mellow background were the green motionless leaves of the young maples. Within the frame of the picture, which in its entirety seemed more like a painting by one of the old masters than a scene on an Iowa farm in the nineteenth century, Phyllis's matchless figure and strangely beautiful face, surmounted by the sweeping curve of the sombrero and bathed in a nimbus of light, held her father spell bound.

Her hair, which was of the deepest shade of coppery brown, a color that one comes across once, perhaps, in a lifetime, lay in heavy short waves about her low forehead. The eyebrows, which were but slightly arched, though unusually thick, were delicately pencilled, and, like the eyelashes, were, if possible, a still darker shade than her hair. The long, straight lashes, if anything, turned downward rather than outward, and gave to the large, dark, courageous violet eyes a lovable and deeply pathetic look. A nose by no means small but straight and regular, indicating sensitiveness with much determination, was set above a not overshort upper lip, which formed in conjunction with the full, rich, red ripeness of its lower neighbor, and its moist, bow-like outlines, the sweetest, firmest, softest, most masterful, yet most alluring and seductive mouth ever given to woman to encompass man's surrender. As for her complexion, it was of that transparent, creamy-white that is sometimes found in certain kinds of sea shells, slightly glazed. A suspicion of crushed rose leaves underlaid its smoothness. In the matter of symmetry

and physical points, she would have discounted an
artist's model, while with all her rare gifts of
mind and body, she was every inch a woman,
and with a full measure of the complex vagaries
of her sex.

"What do I think of it?" said Hartland,
"why, it suits you admirably."

And then after a pause, "Do you know you are
a very handsome woman, Phyllis?"

"Handsome is as handsome does," she replied
with an irresistibly arch look. "Wouldn't you
rather I were good?"

"You are both," said he. "How can I reward
you? I was just thinking when you came in sight,
how much I owed both you and Ruth for the disappointment and heartbreaks that I have caused
you. But times I fully believe will brighten. Of
course, the wheat is not all I expected it would be,
but we'll have some good growing showers yet,
and they'll help it out wonderfully. Indeed, I
shouldn't wonder if it rained tonight."

They looked out through the gap in the woods.
The wind had died completely away. The calm,
born of intense heat had settled upon prairie and
wheatfield. The sky was a sheet of pale, burnished
brass. Not a cloud speck flecked its brazen surface. No one but a man blind to everything but
his own wishes could have extracted a crumb of
comfort out of the situation. A cactus could not
have desired anything drier. The earth gasped,
and even the grasshoppers that burrowed in the
burning sand were too hot to call to each other
with their usual rasping creaks. The Osage river
was no longer a river; it dragged its turbid and

complaining course through muddy shoals and yellow sand-bars. The bluff that sheltered Hartland and his daughter was as the shadow of a rock in a dry land.

Phyllis's brave eyes filled. Oh, if she could but water the wheatfields with her tears! Then with a smile she reflected it might make them too salty; they were not in their porridge state yet.

"Do n't, do n't build on the rain, father. I mean do n't depend upon it. Miss Tabitha Scrimp told me today, and she knows lots about such things — she 's writing a magazine article on the 'Arid Regions of Nebraska, or What 's the Matter With the Rain?' — and she says we 're in for another long spell of drouth, sure."

"Miss Tabitha humbug!" exclaimed Hartland, "why, she 's in league with that redheaded old brother of hers, the attorney. He 's trying to rob me of Cloverdale and now his sister would like to deprive me of my crops. Do n't believe a word they tell you, my child. They 're all tarred with the same brush, Coboss, Hereford and the whole boiling of them. No, don't tell me," he shouted, his temper rapidly rising, "that Tabitha this, that or the other knows more about the weather prognostications than I do. It 's preposterous! Perhaps she don't know that I pick out the weather charts every day."

"I do not wish to express an opinion just yet about the others," said Phyllis, "but I do know this, father — and understand me, I am in earnest — Tabitha Scrimp is your friend, · rain or no rain,' as Joe Parilla says."

Hartland glanced at his daughter's face, but it

bore a look that rendered further controversy on the subject of Miss Scrimp an impossibility.

"Father," said Phyllis, presently, "will you please tell me for my own heart's ease, how much do you owe Colonel Coboss, I mean on the mortgage?"

"Why certainly, child," and it was the first time he had ever conceded or vouchsafed so much, "the balance owing is twenty-five hundred dollars."

"Thanks, daddy, and when has it to be paid?"

"Oh, not all at once, five equal instalments, half yearly."

"And when are you going to give him some more money?"

"I pay him the next instalment on the 10th of September."

"But where is the money coming from?"

"Phyllis, dear, I have ample at my credit in the bank to meet this payment and all other pressing demands until I realize on the crop. The heaviest tax then will be the retiring the notes held by the machinery men, and the liquidating the bank advances made to meet the farm expenses, secured in part by the crop. If the crop fails me, I shall have nothing, however, to carry on the war with next spring."

"Yes, you will," said Phyllis, like a flash, "I know someone who will never fail you."

"Who?" asked Hartland.

"God!" said Phyllis.

The boldness of the answer set Hartland thinking.

"I thought Colonel Coboss's mortgage covered the crops?" said Phyllis.

"Hardly," said her father, "I let them draw the papers pretty much as they pleased, but I constituted the crop the 'dead line'."

The ravishing bow formed by Phyllis's two lips suddenly contracted until they resembled a hollow rosebud, when a dainty inflation of the cheeks was followed by the exclamation, "Phew!"

A golden oriole at this moment dashed across the path pursued by a screaming blue jay and left for an instant a beam as if from a rainbow on Phyllis's skirt, creating a timely diversion.

"Daddy, dear," she said a moment later, as if inspired with a sudden resolution, "would you mind paying Ruth and me what you say you owe us, tomorrow?"

"No," said Hartland, laughing, "if you will tell me how to do it."

"You promise, then?" said she.

"Faithfully," he replied.

"And won't ask any questions?"

"Not one, if you do n't wish it."

"Well, then, we want twelve pigs, smallish, you know, with curly tails, Berkshires; fifty cocks and hens, Hamburghs and Plymouth Rocks; five acres of the home paddock for our own special use; a man once in a while to' do some odd chores for us; and two grade cow-ow-ows." The last word musically prolonged on a chromatic scale in Phyllis's deepest contralto.

"Great heavens!" exclaimed her father, honestly agitated, and jumping up from the fallen tree trunk, "have you no consideration for —"

"For my father's promise?" interrupted Phyllis. "Yes, father, the greatest; and for that very reason I won't let you be untrue to yourself. Remember you said 'faithfully' with a great big 'F'."

"'No, don't tell me,'" she continued in a deep bass voice, imitating his own style, and borrowing the phraseology he had himself used when he was declaiming against Tabitha Scrimp, then kissing him again and again, and breaking into a low ripple of the most infectious laughter, in which even for his very life's sake, he couldn't help but join, she felt she had him in perfect control.

"Now after me," she said, and pitching her voice, so that the trees acknowledged her presence, she commenced intoning the word "faith-ful-ly;" when he, recognizing his defeat, and seized with the absurdity of the situation, followed her example.

Then, arm in arm, while the shadows fell on sere prairie and parched wheatfield, on dusty bluff and thirsty valley, with lighter hearts than they had had for many a day, Hartland and Phyllis marched toward the bungalow hilariously chanting their ridiculous refrain.

CHAPTER VIII

Sarza Denounces Jonas Scrimp.

When Sarza tapped Jonas Scrimp on the shoulder, warned him to silence by her finger on her lips, and led the way to her own apartments, the little rufous headed lawyer could hardly suppress his agitation.

Without ever having acquired the requisite amount of nervous courage necessary to enable him to make a declaration, he felt tolerably convinced that the inherent ardor that was consuming him could not by any possibility have escaped the notice of the "genuine woman," who regulated the interior economy of Maverick Hall.

He had time and again detected her in the act of casting lightning flashes upon him from her black electric eyes. As these glances were invariably accompanied by a faint smile — of a peculiar quality, perhaps, but yet a smile — it required little judicial reasoning on his part to convince himself that he had succeeded in inspiring in the ample bosom of the inflammable creole, a counterpart of the passion that was raging in his own breast. His legal mind, however, had hitherto taught him to refrain from any open manifestation. His professional instincts which dominated — so he admitted to himself in the privacy of his chamber — even the dictates of his bursting heart, urged him to permit the enemy — no, hardly that, the opposite side —

to show its hand first. This view of the situation, coupled perhaps with constitutional nervousness, had hitherto alone prevented him from unburdening his mind. The proper moment, however, had at last almost providentially, it seemed, presented itself, and without any active effort on his part. The first advance had actually come from the other side. He could scarcely believe his eyes.

With rather hazy notions of the code of gallantry or the permissible limits extended to lovers, his wildest expectations, he reasoned, were destined to be more than realized. He was a little agitated, it must be admitted, and while the bowness of his slender legs made the knocking together of his knees a physical impossibility, his heart beat like a trip-hammer. He tried to recall his sister Tabitha's remarks on the occasion of a "small and early" when she coyly ventured the opinion in the presence of Jim Hereford and others, that "women adored a bold lover and scorned a timid one," and so nerved himself for action.

Entering the doorway of the housekeeper's parlor, his plan was momentarily checked by a footstool, with which he became entangled. This, while an undignified and embarrassing episode, as he afterwards remembered, when the incidents of that memorable day rose before him in the white light of recollection, did not, however, deter him. Like Bonaparte, or a snail on a garden path, a course once determined upon, no obstacle he professed to believe could divert him from his purpose.

As Sarza closed the door and turned to confront him, he, fully confident that she was eagerly awaiting his long delayed declaration, and marveling why fate had singled him out from among all the throng of ambitious men in Broncho County to become the repository of her affections, seized her hand and drawing her towards him, ere she had time to divine his intention, imprinted a resounding kiss on her plump cheek.

" Sarza," he said, " I've waited long for this."

Now if a thunderbolt had fallen and had demolished the entire state of Iowa, it would not have caused one half the surprise or amazement in the mind of the Louisianian as did Jonas Scrimp's unwarrantable effrontery.

Sarza's blood rose to the boiling point.

" You have waited long for this, have you?" she screamed as she recovered her lost presence of mind and her breath.   " You infernal scoundrel, how dare you? But you shan't wait much longer," and seizing the no less astonished but more terrified Jonas by the throat, she shook him with the united strength of her " heft " and her indignation until his goggles fell upon the carpet, and his red locks waved widely about his unpleasant looking face, now rapidly becoming purple.

" You would, would you?" she said, jerking him this way and that way as a child would shake a rag baby, finally throwing him on a lounge with considerable violence but with little perceptible effort of her round, supple arms, where he lay the picture of humiliation, contrite and broken.

" Believe me Miss, that is, Madam, I mean Mademoiselle Sarza"—to this day never having determined her legal status—" I, I intended no disrespect. I was carried away by, by my fe—feelings," he half sobbed, " I hum—humbly appo—pologize," and he replaced the green goggles which she handed to him, and bowed his head, the picture of abject woe. Then, looking up, " Will you forgive me?" he said.

" Jonas Scrimp," replied Sarza, now in full possession of her faculties and perfect mistress of the situation, her look of intense indignation giving way to one of smiling contempt, " I always knew you were a knave, but I never suspected you were a fool."

Jonas winced.

" Yes," she continued, " I'll forgive you, and as I think we ought to understand each other a little better" (it occurred to Scrimp if they didn't understand each other now, what further treatment might there be in store for him), " complete frankness on my part is now in order, for you have nobly absolved me," and this with an unmistakable accent, "from any delicacy I might have felt out of consideration for your feelings."

The wretched little man bent his head yet lower.

" I am not in the habit of picking my words, Mr. Scrimp," she went on, " I called you a scoundrel and a knave, either is good enough for the purpose, let it go at that. You are entitled to know my justification for using the epithets. Stand up."

He stood, obedient as a school boy. The bow of his black necktie was under his ear. The bosom of his white shirt front was no longer immaculate. His collar hung by a single buttonhole. His natty office suit fitted him like a sack. He had the appearance of a man who had been drawn through a mangle. Had he been about to be lynched he could not have presented a more truly melancholy spectacle.

"Jonas Scrimp, you are a forger!" The attorney's face grew green, then white, then purple. He was on the verge of vertigo. His power of speech forsook him, he could merely wave his hand in feeble protest.

"You inserted in the instrument or mortgage, or whatever you call it, that was given by Laban Hartland as security for the loan advanced him by my master, a clause, after the document had been duly signed, which gave the holder of that mortgage the additional power to foreclose if deemed advisable upon the standing crops and implements and farm stock, as well as upon the land. There was no collusion on Colonel Coboss's part. You and Dago Phil were the sole instigators of your own knavery. No! No! it's useless to attempt to deny it, I hold the proof!"

But Scrimp, while he heard the scathing denunciation, and recognized the truth of the arraignment, was in no condition to either deny or assent. He was suffering from syncope. Not wanting to complicate matters by having a fainting attorney on her hands, and her womanly nature responding to the mute appeal, Sarza rushed to the buffet for a glass of spirits. No further word passed between them, but when Jonas had sufficiently revived, and was arranging his toilet preparatory to leaving, as crestfallen a wooer and as thoroughly frightened a pettifogger as it is possible to conceive, Sarza stooped and whispered in his ear: "Remember, Jonas Scrimp," she said, "I shall

watch your further proceedings with the keenest
interest."

The mortified attorney vouchsafed no answer,
but hurried from the housekeeper's room.

    *   *   *   *   *   *

CHAPTER IX.

Phyllis Listens to a Declaration.

The dramatic incidents of the day, however, were not permitted to end with the lawyer's exit, for as he turned into the vestibule of the hall, he almost fell into the arms of Phyllis Hartland, who, equipped in riding habit and sombrero and humming the air of a plantation song, came bounding through the doorway.

"Oh! I beg your pardon, Mr. Scrimp," said Phyllis, as she encountered the unfortunate man squarely with her hundred and fifty pounds of buoyant virility, "we didn't see each other, did we?"

But Scrimp, usually so obsequious and unpleasantly polite, paid no attention to her courtesy, and fled the scene.

"What in the world was the matter with Jonas Scrimp today?" she asked later, as over a cup of tea in the housekeeper's room, she related the story of their meeting. "He was downright rude, though I must say I prefer his silence to his compliments."

"I think he was a little upset today," replied Sarza with the faintest twinkle in her eye, which Phyllis, being a remarkably observant young person, did not fail to detect.

They had much to talk about, indeed they never met without exchanging many confidences.

Both of a keenly sympathetic nature, and each with a manner that inspired unbounded trust in the other, they were wont to lay bare the ordinary secrets of their lives with little reserve. Sarza's natural brightness, shrewd common-sense, wide experience, and maturer years instinctively excited Phyllis's admiration and respect; while Phyllis's magnetic personality, brilliant mental gifts, her youth, her goodness and her beauty encouraged the creole woman to regard her almost in the light of a divinity.

The conversation turned upon the determination by Phyllis unknown to her father, to enter the ranks of the breadwinners and the scope and success of her efforts, — a work that she had entered upon and prosecuted with the enthusiasm of a new convert.

It had taken her but a short time, after the arrival of herself and Ruth at Cloverdale, to realize that the blind infatuation that possessed Laban Hartland to cultivate wheat to the exclusion of all other crops, and to ignore corn or cattle, the two safest and most profitable branches of agricultural industry for that section of the country, could only end in defeat and loss. She further quickly grasped the fact that the construction of the over elaborate barns, windmills, granary, stables and dwelling, to say nothing of the purchase of farm stock and machinery and three years' working expenses, apart from the purchase of the property itself, must have all but exhausted the capital that her father brought with him from Massachusetts.

With no definite aim at first, beyond the dis-

taste of leading an idle life, and the characteristic
desire to have something to occupy her spare
hours, she finally determined when she foresaw
that the need might arise at any moment for every
dollar, nay, every cent, to turn to practical account the advantages that a first class education had
conferred upon her. She had fully counted upon
being entrusted with the management at least of
the dairy, and the poultry, and her astonishment
was unbounded when she found that her father
had actually carried his threat againt the "prong
horned brutes" into execution. Her field of useful-
ness being burked in this direction, she had confided her perplexities to Sarza, who not only cor-
dially endorsed her plans, but at once set to work
among her Broncho City acquaintances to promote
the scheme.

Few difficulties were encountered. Indeed, it
only needed to be hinted that the handsome Miss
Hartland from Massachusetts was prepared to give
instruction in singing, music, physical culture and
Delsarte, than the upper crust of that great cattle
centre, so to speak, "fell over one another" in
their haste to secure the services of so cultured a
person, and embrace the opportunity that would
doubtless lead to closer social relations.

Miss Tabitha Scrimp who was really a very
kind hearted soul, and knew or was known by
almost every one in the county, overwhelmingly
impressed with Phyllis's highbred but unaffected
ways, was the first to "set the pace."

"Mr. Hereford told me, my dear," said she
addressing Phyllis, "that all my voice requires is
a little more 'timbre', timber, you know." And

she piped a treble little laugh at her own conceit.
" I am sure you could help me out with my favorite song. Mr. Hereford says he's certain it must
be all the rage in Boston. It commences,

     '**Guardilquiver gen-tle re-vir,**'"

and she shook her small red head with its un-
matched locks, until the parti-colored ringlets
danced a ludicrous accompaniment.

Lena, Miss Scrimp's " hired girl," envious of
the obvious improvement in her mistress's style
and dying to appear fully up to date in the eyes of
Dago Phil, her lover, also pleaded for tuition and
got it. Phyllis was too thorough a lady to draw a
social line, she only insisted that her clients should
be well washed and respectable. Her services
were soon in such demand that she had to refuse
many unfortunate suppliants, for with her splendid and gracious ways she had won the hearts of
the entire country side.

Even Cornelius Kobb, an individual most par-
simonious in his praise, was heard to declare for
the edification of a crowd of cattlemen waiting for
the mail, inspired possibly by the picture of Phyllis,
who was a superb horsewoman, galloping past on
her big sorrel mare, " that gal o' ole man Hartland
wuz clar out o' sight."

Phyllis, however, was not satisfied. Though
calisthenics, music and singing proved a pleasant
and easy enough way of making money, it was all
on so small a scale, that the spirit of acquisition
which presently possessed her, made her heart-sick
of her feeble methods. With all her higher education and refinement, she was gifted with plenty of
common-sense — " horse sense," Joe Parilla called

it — and good business abilities. She was convinced that in some direction or other, an opportunity was waiting for her through which she could be of substantial aid to her father, and while praying for guidance took great care to keep her beautiful eyes very wide open.

A "straight tip" as Ruth expressed it, soon came and from a most unexpected quarter. Almost all the butter, milk and eggs consumed at Cloverdale by the family and farm hands was purchased from Cornelius Kobb, and it was one of Phyllis's self-imposed daily duties to drive over in the buckboard and obtain from that proverbially grumpy old granger the regulation rations.

It took but one visit from Phyllis to work the undoing of that worthy man and bring him with the rest of the community to her feet. To again borrow from Ruth's vocabulary, "poor old Korn Kobb was completely broken up," and it only required an uplifting of Phyllis's eyebrows, a grateful look from her big violet eyes, a parting of her rose-leaf lips, a sudden gleam of her milk-white teeth, and a simple "Good morning, Mr. Kobb," and the whole thing was accomplished. Indeed, on more than one occasion quite a display of temper was exhibited by the angular mother of Mr. Kobb's numerous offspring. The liberal measure of dairy products he was in the habit, when not closely watched, of bestowing upon Phyllis, aroused that good lady's suspicions, and later, their custody passed entirely out of his keeping. The patronage vested in the eggs, however, yet remained in his hands, and he seldom neglected, if hidden from the cat-like observation of Mrs. Kobb's gimlet-like eyes, to place an extra egg or so in Phyllis's basket. His suggestion therefore one day that Phyllis should "git the 'ole man to buy her some hins, a few shoats and tew or three coows, and I kin drap arcound onst in a while and size up the aouttit," as it was manifestly to his own pecuniary disadvantage, must have been surely due to his wish to "git squar with the ole woman."

It was this suggestion that had induced Phyllis to wait upon Sarza in such hot haste, and seek the benefit of her judgment.

"An excellent idea," said she, when Phyllis had unfolded her plan, "and good money in it. Besides you see, my dear child, you will still have time to devote to the most profitable of your pupils. O, yes! you must not move a step without first telling your father. See him this very afternoon. No fear! you can win him over. Only get him committed to a distinct promise before you breathe the word 'cow.' I look upon this, if you succeed, as of course you will, as the thin end of the wedge. You dear thing, you'll overcome all his objections in time, if you'll only keep up your patience and courage. I know it's rank treason even to whisper it, but we'll make a dairyman of your father yet."

Then they kissed, and Phyllis hastened to mount her slashing sorrel mare and start for home.

Deep in reflection as she cantered along the yielding prairie trail, she failed to hear the hoof beats of a spirited chestnut thoroughbred that was suddenly reined up alongside her. With a start she raised her head and encountered the gaze of Colonel Coboss's piercing black eyes.

"Pardon me, Miss Hartland," said the Colonel

in a somewhat agitated voice, accompanied by a
deferential sweep of his wide white panama, "I
fear I startled you. Truth is, I could hardly hold
Caliph in," and he patted the neck of the magnificent animal, now tightly reined and champing fret-
fully at the bit.

"Indeed, Colonel," said Phyllis, "then your
arms need some physical culture," and she smiled
contrary to her will, "for you ride with a cruel
enough bit."

"Your remark gives me the opportunity I
sought," he replied, his voice still trembling, "O,
Miss Hartland! for God's sake give up physical
culture! I rode —"

He paused for a moment. All manner of con-
jectures floated through Phyllis's brain. Was he
mad? Had he been drinking? A glance showed
that he was rational, though in a fever of excitement. What then, could he mean? Before she
could utter the bantering reply upon her lips, as to
whether he would prefer her to give him lessons in
deportment, he had grasped the mare's bridle and
checking his own horse to a standstill, with a
touch of the spur had swung its head in the opposite direction and sat in his saddle facing her.

"I rode after you on purpose to say this," he
went on, speaking more and more excitedly. "I
heard of it today for the first time. I beseech of
you, Miss Hartland, to give the whole thing up,
music, singing and all the rest of it. Your, your
position demands it. Your, your hands were not
intended to sew buttons. Let me have the right,
I entreat of you, dear, dear Phyllis, to —"

But he got no further. Indeed, he had gone

too far. Compulsory love-making, he must understand, was not to Phyllis's taste.

"Stop," she said, the half wondering smile giving way to a look of sudden resentment, "your
motives, Colonel Coboss, may be distinctly praise-
worthy, but your actions, sir, are not those of a
gentleman. Release my bridle!" And with a cut
of her whip across Starlight's flanks, and a faint
inclination of her head in the direction of the now
furious master of Maverick Hall, she rode away
into the sunset.

But it was ordained that Phyllis was not even
yet to reach her destination that fateful evening
without further incident. More nettled than indignant at the display of Colonel Coboss's interest
in her private affairs, but disgusted and perhaps
wounded more than she cared to admit, at the
awkwardness of his ill-timed declaration, she
vented her pique with another slash of the whip on
the mare's sorrel shoulders.

She sought, unconsciously to herself, an opportunity for reflection. The quiet of the Cloverdale
woods instinctively possessed her mind. A glance
over her shoulder revealed the still motionless
figure of the Colonel and his big chestnut dimly
outlined against the rippling horizon, the cloud of
dust raised by Starlight's heels gradually obliterat-
ing the picture.

Anxious to make the shortest cut for home, she
left the trail, and turning the mare's head rode in
a bee-line across the prairie in the direction of a
small bluff, beyond which the smoke of the bungalow at Cloverdale was picturesquely visible, as
it spiralled its blue way against the brazen western

sky. As she skirted alongside the bight of this intervening bluff, and checked the mare's pace for fear of throwing her by reason of the wild vines that trailed among the longer grass, a big man on a tall, black horse galloped suddenly out of a gap in the chaparral, and rode out to intercept her.

For one brief second, her heart — she was a woman after all — gave an almost imperceptible bound, next a small sigh escaped her, whether of relief, disappointment or weariness, it is hard to say—the moment after, Black Jim Hereford, with a reverent doff of his broad plainsman's hat, ranged up alongside her.

"Pardon, Miss Hartland," he said, "for so rudely startling you, and forgive me when I admit that I am no better than a road agent. I have been lying in wait for you."

"Your boldness, Mr. Hereford, is almost on a par with your candor." She said this smiling, the faintest possible suspicion of restraint visible. "Perhaps you think that either one condones the other, or your own admission negatives both?"

"Hardly that," replied the swarthy young giant, "your powers of reasoning are too subtle for me."

"I half expected," she said, "when I first saw you emerging from the shadow of the wood that it was a case of money or my life, and was considering whether I ought to trust myself to Starlight or to you, though I was quite prepared to throw up my hands and surrender."

"Would you really have done so?"

"Indeed, I would."

"Had I believed that, Miss Phyllis, I should humbly have demanded it."

"What, my poor little purse?"

"No, your life."

"This is really too much," she said to herself, "and all in one day," then aloud, "Now, Mr. Hereford, you are sanguinary. Remember," she added, laughing, "I also carry a gun."

"I am not jesting," he replied, earnestly.

She stooped and ran her fingers through the mare's mane.

"I would rather you had thrown up your hands, I wanted your life in trust."

"Now, you are getting hopelessly mixed," she said.

He was treading on dangerous ground and knew it. Not daring to challenge an issue yet, he changed his tone.

"Your father," he went on, "is in difficulties, Miss Hartland. I have learned of your noble self-sacrifice. Don't think me presumptuous. The honor of such a brief acquaintance as ours does not, I know, warrant me in exercising the privileges of an old friend, but the thought of your having to sew on 'buttons' makes me —"

"Not quite as bad as that, Mr. Hereford, she interrupted, laughing aloud. "I and my sister have been making badges for the cattlemen, and pin money for ourselves. What are you, a 'G.' 'J.' or 'S' man?" And before he could reply, she went on, "it is so kind of you to think about our affairs, and I don't mind making a confidant of you. I am giving all these lessons in music and calisthenics quite unknown to my father, and in order to carry out a little scheme of my own. Will you respect my secret?" and she held out a firm, white hand.

The touch thrilled him and rendered him for the minute perfectly irresponsible, and she, realizing the danger of delay, and ere he had time to frame a reply, placed her finger to her lips, touched Starlight smartly with the whip and once more wheeled and rode away into the heart of the August sunset.

CHAPTER X

In the Coteau of the Missouri.

Dr. Maryann St. Lambert was an extensive breeder of beef cattle. Indeed, in the matter of the extent of his cattleruns and the numerical vastness of his sleek herds, he was a formidable rival of Colonel Coboss. Beyond the fact that they were both enthusiastic stockmen, and were both reputedly of great wealth, they had but little else in common. St. Lambert, though a clever exponent of the healing art, for so young a man, had but recently surrendered a lucrative practice in the east. This he had done in prompt accordance with the terms of his uncle's will which made it compulsory for him to devote his undivided time to the management of the magnificent estate of which he had suddenly found himself the lucky possessor.

Upon the acquisition of the property and the inheritance of so much available wealth, a goodly share of convertible stocks and bonds being also included in the windfall, he set himself conscientiously to work to carry out the terms of the inheritance. These conditions, as imposed by the last will and testament of the late Hugo Maryann, though obligatory, were not in the least unreasonable. They merely provided that the incoming heir should expend a certain sum annually in the way of experiments and tests, with representatives

and acknowledged breeds of beef and dairy cattle.
Being from the very nature of his profession of a
scientific and analytic turn of mind, St. Lambert
proceeded to carry out the wishes of his enterpris-
ing kinsman with an energy and broadness of purpose that were his chief characteristics.

He started in by experimenting with purely
beef cattle, with a view to determine what breed
of animals under similar given conditions would
ultimately "weigh in" best. A most necessary
branch of investigation, in view of the fact that the
price of beef at this time at the great urban centers
of trade, was lower than it had been for years.
When this line of inquiry had practically material-
ized and the process of breeding and development
of competing grades of beef animals was in active
operation, he turned his attention to the selection
of dairy stock. The annual value of the national
exports of the product of the dairy, he said, could
reasonably be doubled. "Instead of ten, it should
be twenty million dollars."

But the question of the quality of the milk
raised for home consumption he maintained was in
reality of more importance than the quality of even
beef or flour raised for the same purpose. Milk,
he used to declare, not wheat, was the backbone of
the country. What did the babies or the sick people want with bread without butter. Rich milk
was manifestly the proper diet for the infant generation. And the richer it was, naturally the more
adulteration it would stand. With this manner of
argument, and in his own frank, hearty way, he
would laughingly combat the contentions of Laban
Hartland, whom as a wheat bigot, he lightly accused

of being in collusion with the great cereal operators on the Chicago Board of Trade.

"What would your little granddaughter, Daisy, do, eh, Mr. Hartland, without her daily allowance of fresh Cushla cream?"

Holding these views, it was not therefore surprising that St. Lambert should have secured for experimental purposes some of the choicest animals that money could procure, or that among their number, some Guernseys and dove-colored Jerseys were not the least prominent.

"Daddy," said Ruth Hartland, dashing into her father's office one bright, breezy morning, shortly after the incidents related in the preceeding chapter, "Dr. St. Lambert is here and you have to come."

Laban, who was in a brown study, was trying to prove to his own satisfaction that the deposit of fertile drift which lay thick on the coteau of the Missouri, could never be impoverished by the successive cropping of wheat.

"Yes! you have to come, dear old dad. Throw away that musty book. This is the day, the long looked for day for the long promised visit to Cushla Range, and it has been a mighty long time coming. Everyone is going, Dorothy and Daisy, Phyllis of course, and Sarza. Mr. Hereford drove her over this morning, but he wouldn't even come in. Joe Parilla is going to take the big army wagon and four horses, and drive you all but me."

"And pray what's 'me' going to do?" asked her father, aroused against his will.

"O, I'm going—at least Dr. St. Lambert has invited me to drive with him in his new buckboard—if I may?"

Ruth, though of a somewhat different type, was quite as distinguished a specimen of femininity as her sister. Exceptionally tall, an inch taller than Phyllis, to whom in some respects she bore a striking similarity, she yet possessed certain characteristics of mind and body exclusively her own. She was a brunette with a clear, dazzling complexion and great masses of rich brown hair, which in short curls clustered about her forehead. This striking combination, together with a pair of big, luminous grey eyes and a mobile, mischievous face, variable and full of expression, produced an impression of beauty, more charming than mere possession of regularity of feature. Though unusually tall, her willowy figure and slender hands and feet were the personification of grace. Added to this, a buoyant temperament rendered her a dangerously fetching type of lovable girlhood.

It is needless to say that her father surrendered.

The order of the "going" was carried out strictly upon the lines as laid down by Ruth. Leading the way was the unpainted buckboard drawn by two rangy bays, while on the luxuriously cushioned seat, snuggling quite unnecessarily close to the doctor, sat the self-constituted mistress of ceremonies, "herself." On the box seat of the big Concord wagon was perched Joe Parilla, handling the reins, and soothing with many a "so-ho" and "whoa there, pet"—not the smiling Sarza seated by his side—but the team of four spanking grays that were pawing and sneezing, inspired by the cool air of early morning. In the middle seat sat Mrs. Dorothy Dean and little Daisy, while in the seat behind was Phyllis by her father's side,

with the double object of not sharing with Joe,
Sarza's divided attention, and the better to divert
Hartland's mind from the study of wheat, to the
contemplation of cattle.

The prairie trail was perfection and under Joe's
control — he was a skilled whip, and could handle
a four-in-hand as easily as he could a "jerk-line"
outfit or a "string-team" — they bowled merrily
along. It was in the first freshness of the morning, and they inhaled the ozone, damp with last
night's baptism of merciful dew, and aromatic
with the perfume of the few wild flowers that
were blinking their half open eyes at the slowly
mounting sun. Behind them this same rising sun
was tinting with a narrow selvedge of gold the
turquoise peaks of the distant Sweet Grass Hills,
and embossing with braids of glory the rust brown
banks of the Osage river. Into the valley of this
with locked wheels they later descended and
forded the stream where, though the river was
deeper, its bed was not yielding sand. Here the
horses plunged for a footing on the stony bottom
in water almost to their bellies and which whipped
treacherously around their legs, the spray of it
being thrown up in clouds that glistened in the
sunshine, and danced away down stream to Daisy's
admiration.

Out on the plateau again, scorched relics of
wild flowers confronted them on every side, their
grass-grey stems with yet greyer crests, waving
their fading possibilities of crimson and yellow,
blue, orange and white. Under ordinary circumstances, these sun kissed plains would have presented in their summer glory flaming contrasts

with the parti-colored circles of luxuriant sedge grass which spread in varying rings around them. Evidence of the universal drouth was everywhere omnipotent, its effects, as Hartland was not slow to notice, not being confined exclusively to his own doomed wheat fields. To this he drew Phyllis's attention.

"See," he said, "the stockmen whom you are never tired of inviting me to imitate, are in as dire straits as am I."

There was justification for his stricture. The uplands where they had escaped the prevailing fires were in many places a yellow-russet color, scarred, however, in every direction, with huge wastes of uninviting blackness, the ebon legacy of the devastating flames, which had draped countless acres of once verdant plain in sombre sackcloth and ashes.

"Quite true," said Phyllis, "but only in a limited degree. The prairie, unlike your poor wheat fields, is not altogether unfruitful. The vastness of the ranges permits, of course, a proportion of good grazing ground."

"Supposing Cloverdale was converted into a grazing ground," he urged, "it would be no more fertile than it is as a wheat farm."

"You are mistaken, father," she said, "while the drouth has proved fatal to the heading out of your grain, it has not prevented your raising any quantity of stalk, capital fodder, but you have no stock to feed it to. Besides, the prairie is not all withered up, it has been over-run by fires. Look!"

They had cleared the point of a wooded island, and before them, in spectacular contrast, stretched

and stretched an apparently limitless tract of luxuriant meadow land, the physical contour of which,
with its undulations, suggested the unbroken bil-
lows of a ground-swell that one is apt to encounter
off an ocean headland before a storm.

CHAPTER XI

The Great Cushla Cattle Range.

St. Lambert had reined up his horses and the four-in-hand drew up alongside.

"I have been telling Miss Ruth," said he, "that I have been trying to arrange a little surprise for you. It is not the season for a 'round-up' and it is not altogether the best thing for the cattle, but as Hardisty said that he'd assume all responsibilities, my scruples vanished. You will only see the beef cattle, though not all of them; several thousand head, perhaps. The dairy animals we will see later."

"I am just dying," said Phyllis, "to see a real big mob of cattle. My experience so far has been limited to scattered bunches. How much farther do we go?"

"Only a mile or so."

"There's no danger, doctor?" asked Mrs. Dean, hugging Daisy closer.

"Not a bit," said he, "as long as you stick to the wagon, but they'd horn you to a certainty if you were on foot."

"Ah! Ah! Miss Ruthie, do you hear that, now?" said Laban Hartland, who had been waiting for just such an opportunity to pour in some hot shot, and here at the last moment, and on the battle ground, as it were, one of his strongest contentions against the bossy brutes was confirmed by

the highest authority. " I have always maintained
these prong horned devils are not safe to handle."

"Neither is wheat, daddy dear." said Ruth,
" when there are thistles in it." This very sweetly
but with mischievous inflection.

They had reached a cup-like basin at the foot of
a low range of hills. Beyond an intervening lake-
let they could now discern acres of animal life,
instinct with motion. On nearer approach, this
motion was found to be progressive and slowly
moving in a swaying sort of way. An agitated
ocean of red-brown waves, flecked with froth. A
huge carpet of hides shaken by giants. As they
drove yet nearer, a sea of tossing horns became
visible, and the spirit of the crusader again arose
in Hartland's breast.

" If those beasts were mine, St. Lambert," he
said, " which God forbid, I'd dehorn them."

The doctor exchanged glances with Ruth.
" Yes, there's something in that, Mr. Hartland,"
said the doctor, smiling, " but there would be no
money in it. As a business man, you'll appreciate
that view of it."

What more could Laban say?

When within a hundred yards or so, individual
animals could be distinguished as they moved round
about the outskirts of the herd. Before them
" rounded up" in a compact mass quietly munching away at the rich pasture at their feet or gazing
excitedly with heads tossed wildly in the air at the
advancing carriages, or in the case of the outside
ones, circling around the almost immovable centre,
like the outer eddies of a vast whirlpool — stood
thousands of head of restless cattle. Cows and bulls,

steers and calves, every variety of reds, whites,
browns and blacks with coats like satin, and notwithstanding the alleged poverty of pasture, rolling
fat.

Even Hartland was stirred with enthusiasm
despite his stubborn will, for his shrewd eye detected a percentage of muley cows, and he grasped
at the excuse as a drowning man would at a straw.

"Quite a band, quite a band, doctor," said he,
"I am glad you do n't insist on horns in all cases.
Must be a lot of money there."

"You 're right, and the beauty of it is, sir, that
the calves head out without rain."

"Yes, but they need milk," said Laban.

"Quite so," replied the doctor, "but we do n't
water it."

"But you have to water the cows, doctor,"
chuckled the wheat king.

"True," retorted St. Lambert, "but we take
them to the 'crick'; you can't do that, you know,
with your wheat fields."

Hartland's jaw fell; like a wise general he
knew when he was defeated.

"How many head altogether?" asked Phyllis.

"Hardisty will have to answer," said the doctor. "I 'll hail him," and putting his fingers to his
lips, blew three shrill whistles.

At rest and very statuesquely bunched together
some two hundred yards away, half a dozen cowboys were lounging in their saddles.

Phyllis, who was steeped to the very lips in her
love for the picturesque, revelled in the scenic
effect. The lowing, slowly moving herd; the hill-
protected valley; the miles of billowy sward,

saturated with varying shades of green, as the early sunbeams peeped over the purple ridges; the strands of gossamer gemmed with dew that floated over the grass like a silver net; the diaphanous banks of mist that hung reluctantly about the reedy shoreline of the shallow lake.

In answer to the shrill drawn-out whistle of the doctor, a member of the band of cowboys, mounted on a big mud-colored broncho, with the long, loping gait peculiar to the Montana breed, detached himself from the group and cantered up to the party. Without him, the picture would have been incomplete.

The rider was as typical and powerful in his way as the animal he rode. Fully six feet when he stood in his stirrups, deep chested, with shoulders not too broad for symmetry, he was built on the lines of an athlete. His legs were encased in leather chaperajos, whose long split fringes looked like a tangle of weeds. His navy blue flannel shirt was open at the throat, and beneath the collar around the neck a deep crimson scarf was tied in a loose sailor knot. His clay colored felt sombrero had a brown leather strap and buckle in place of hat band and was "stayed" with a leather boot lace. A cartridge belt with navy revolver adorned his waist. As he reined up alongside the wagon, he raised his hat and remained for some moments with his head uncovered.

"I think you all know Mr. Hardisty," said the doctor.

They all did. Some more, some less. Among the latter was Phyllis.

As he sat there erect in the saddle, with the

soft light of the morning sun burnishing his golden hair and deeply tanned face, his soft tawney beard and wavy moustache. Phyllis, with her artistic instinct, felt she had never seen so magnificent a looking man. "As for his eyes," she confided by letter to a friend in Boston, "they are of the deepest sea gray, wide open and resolute, tender yet fearless, you know what I mean, with dark eyelashes that curl up. His mouth is only matched by his voice, which is sweet enough to woo a bird off a bough. As for his nose, it's as straight as the ten commandments, and I am told that he is as noble and manly as he looks—and I fully believe it."

"There are about twelve thousand head, including calves, Miss Hartland," said Hardisty in answer to her question.

"Those 'muley cows'," he continued, addressing her father, "which take your fancy so much are polled Angus, the rest of the lot are Durhams and Herefords."

"Many thanks for the novel entertainment you have given us, Mr. Hardisty," said Phyllis, "I shall never forget it."

"This is really nothing, after all," he replied, "but perhaps you will be able to see our grand 'round up' and branding in the fall. The band you have seen, though, will give you a basis on which to form an idea of the extent of the cattle trade of the United States. Last year nearly three hundred thousand live head of cattle were shipped to froeign countries. Worth about twenty-six million dollars. Oh, yes! people will eat; the packers shipped over thirty million dollars worth of fresh and preserved beef, besides."

"Not including the 'American hog?'" said Phyllis.

"Not exclusive altogether of that festive beast."

"Did you ever visit the Chicago stock yards?" he asked.

"No, but we got a whiff of them as we passed through, which hardly encouraged us to investigate further."

"If I don't bore you," he went on, "I want to prove what a mere bagatelle our band of cattle is, compared with the droves they handle at those yards. Last year they received three million seven hundred thousand head."

"Say, Hardisty," said Laban Hartland, "you must have been studying the cattle question from an economic standpoint."

"Not exactly," he replied, "but I believe with 'Jim Bludso' that it's well to have a grip on 'the handful of things I know.' As a matter of fact, the dairy animal is my hobby. I am hopelessly in love with the Jersey cow."

"And I want to be," said Phyllis. "I am ready to make love this very moment. O, Mr. Hardisty! Won't you give me a chance?"

"Do you allow that sort of thing, Mrs. Dean?" said the doctor, who, engrossed in conversation with Ruth, had only overheard Phyllis's reply.

"Oh! that's nothing," interjected Hartland, who, much as he admired the doctor, had not quite forgiven him for his victory in their argumentative tilt. "I have made up my mind to allow my daughters to gang their own sweet will in matters of calf love."

For a moment almost everyone felt uncomfort-

able except Laban, though why, none of them
wanted to consider even for an instant.

The silence was broken by Phyllis.

"Yes, my father deserves a medal, Mr. Hardisty. He has actually consented to our having
two of the objectionable breed at Cloverdale. No,
not a word," she said as Laban raised his hand, as
if about to offer an explanation. "And we hope
to have some calves too, some of these days. I am
one of the fraternity now. I'm a cow-boy. Let's
have a 'milk-shake'." And with an indescribably
winning smile, she extended her hand to Jack
Hardisty.

The horses' heads were now turned towards
Cushla Hall, where the breeds that were being
subjected to the pleasant ordeal of experimental
tests, were confined in separate quarters.

"So far," said St. Lambert, "I have not attempted to undertake any practical dairy tests,
neither have we kept any tab on the comparative
product. I am breeding from selected animals
picked up all over the country and when I get
together twenty or thirty of each breed, then I intend simply for my own satisfaction, to start a
series of competitive tests, you know, for milk,
butter and cheese."

"What then?" said Laban.

"Why, whichever kind proves to be the best
all round for dairy purposes, that breed I shall
handle exclusively. Specialties pay, when you
confine yourself to the best in the market."

"Wheat is my specialty. Does it pay?" asked
Hartland.

"That's exactly it," said St. Lambert, "but

pardon me for saying so, you don't seem to appreciate the distinction. Your making wheat your specialty doesn't make wheat a special product. It's a staple, and like most staples, suffers from over-production. Wheat today is almost a glut. In a year or so, it will be produced greatly in excess of the demand. The bottom price has not been reached yet."

"An average crop even at present prices would still yield a profit," maintained Laban.

"No, sir," said the doctor emphatically, "not even if you harvested twenty bushels to the acre on your entire fifteen hundred acres at forty cents. Placing your expenses at ten dollars, you would then be clear out of pocket three thousand dollars."

"That's right," said Joe Parilla, quite unable to control himself.

"It's too great a risk, Mr. Hartland," said Jack Hardisty, "and consequently too much wear and tear on mind and body. You should go in for mixed farming, or bettter still, for something like this," and he threw open the big gates of a spacious barn-yard.

"These are the true mortgage-lifters," and he pointed to a dozen or more Jersey cows with calves at their heels. "In the yard to the right of these are the Guernseys, to the left are the Shorthorns."

The picture was a charming one, the dove-eyed, tan-colored beasts, watching alternately and wistfully, first the visitors, and then the gambols of their clumsily graceful offspring; these, when they were not engaged in absorbing with dripping lips, their mother's milk, were bucking and skipping, and striking as formidable attitudes of defiance as their uncertain legs would permit them.

"The sweet things," said Phyllis and Ruth in a breath.

"I envy you your responsibilities," added the former, as Hardisty continued to give the histories of some of the cows that Phyllis seemed especially interested in.

"Two of the handsomest Shorthorns came from Colonel Coboss's ranche, two of the Guernseys from Mr. Levi P. Morton's Ellerslie Farm in New York, and one of the Jerseys, and this," said Hardisty, "should interest you very much indeed, came originally from the great Hood Farm at Lowell, in your own state, Miss Hartland."

The question of the projected meeting of cattle men at Broncho City was reverted to at lunch time, and it was arranged that all the Hartland people and the "outfit" from Cushla Hall should attend that function in a body.

After luncheon, an inspection of the home farm followed, Hartland, however, excusing himself from further attendance, having discovered on the doctor's bookshelves a work on the "Ancient Wheat-fields of Egypt," in the pages of which he was soon so deeply engrossed as to encourage him again, and audibly, to consign "all prong-horned brutes to the devil." On the plea of Daisy's being tired out, but possibly inspired with deeper motives, Mrs. Dean took advantage of an inviting couch in the cool shade of a "spare-room" and indulged in her regulation forty winks.

This providential chain of circumstances permitted a disposition of the remainder of the allied forces, which they were not slow to profit by.

Sarza and Joe Parilla, under pretext of inspecting the pink-skinned Cheshire pigs, wandered by mistake into a cornpatch, and for several hours gave themselves up as lost. St. Lambert invited Ruth to inspect a wonderful brood of young prairie chickens, but inadvertently strayed into a young grove of sycamores, which by an original system of pruning almost excluded the sunlight, and this curious fact it took him till nearly tea-time to explain to the entire satisfaction of that young lady. As for Phyllis and the man with the sea-gray eyes, they started at his suggestion to see some coyote cubs, whose home was in the cool shades of the waving chaparral on the banks of the river; but the brush was so dense, according to her account, that Mr. Hardisty, familiar as he appeared to be with every nook and hollow in the woods, did not unearth the foxy little rascals until nearly sundown.

The recital at the tea-table of this comedy of errors hardly seemed to Hartland's judicial mind reconcilable with common sense, and he was about to engage in a bantering discussion with St. Lambert as to the remote possibility " even with sun in your eyes, my dear fellow, of mistaking a covey of partridges for a grove of poplars," when it was fortunately announced that the horses were hitched up and the wheels of the Concord wagon were heard crunching on the gravel.

CHAPTER XII

How "Dago Phil" Disturbed the Peace of Crocus Cottage.

Broncho City was in a state of abnormal excitement. The editor of the Rustler, Phineas D. Quad, by the will of the people Judge, by the voice of the people "Jedge," was measureably responsible for this condition of things. For weeks past the columns of this mirror of public opinion, with headlines of startling magnitude and blackness, had been drawing the attention of the cattle men and grangers to the half-page advertisement on the "fourth (and last) page of this edition," inviting "all interested in the improvement of stock to attend the coming congress of the cattle kings."

The appeal of the "Jedge," "jedging" from appearances, was not destined to be in vain. Every one had signified his intention of being present. That is, everyone who could afford to buy a "button," and under the circumstances scarcely anyone had the hardihood to appear on the streets of the debatable city without one. To be seen without a button, even if you did not know a gopher from a maverick, was tantamount to an open insult to the mild mannered cowboys, and an overt act of remissness to be avoided by the law-abiding citizen as he would a pestilence. Indeed, the "button" was a more significant talisman than a bank account. The church member might forget his gun or even his latch-key, but his "button," no! no! heaven prevent such a calamity! The absence of the "button" had finally come to be regarded as an act of such unpardonable omission, that anyone neglecting to adjust this most important adjunct of the toilette and badge of good citizenship, could be visited with swift retributive justice. For instance, if you met a buttonless man parading the street and restrained from shooting him on sight, you could at least menace him with the terrors of an unwritten law. You merely had to touch your own "button," and he had to "do the rest." This represented anything from a milk-shake to a "ten cent straight." This "calling down" and "setting up" was regarded by the citizens of Broncho as an excruciatingly funny jest, and proved as embarrassing to the "stranger within its gates" as to the women who were in no case held exempt from its recognized exactions.

"Jonas," said Miss Scrimp, addressing her brother across the tea-table one evening, a few days preceding the holding of the congress, "speaking of buttons, I never felt so mortified and cheap in all my life, as I did today. I looked and felt almost as bad as you did that last afternoon you spent at Maverick Hall."

The attorney squirmed.

"By the way, you have never told me to this day how you came to be so disgruntled. Well, as I was saying, who should I meet at the very door of Seltzer's drug store but Judge Quad, the Hartland girls and Sarza. What a sweet girl that is! Do you know, brother, I have often thought that there was something more between you and Sarza than you cared to admit."

She paused, and Jonas cast his weak eyes from his plate of canned salmon to the ceiling, and from the ceiling to his tanned shoes, and finally to his sister, in so hunted and pathetic a manner, that as Tabitha, who afterwards repeated with some reservations the incident to Sarza herself, declared it reminded her "for all the world, my dear, of a poor sheep awaiting its turn in the slaughter house; and Jonas, too, who is usually so fresh."

With a ghastly attempt at a knowing smile, which culminated in a fixed grin, almost as green as his glasses, and with colorless lips drawn tightly across his interrupted, and not too white, teeth, the unfortunate little man seemed bereft of the power of speech. If he did make reply, it was lost in the depths of his coffee cup.

"Ah, ha!" thought Tabitha, whose ferret-like eyes permitted little to escape them, "so that's the way the cat jumps," and then the knowledge of the consecration of her own virgin affections, and the seeming hopelessness of her own aspirations, overcame her, and she added with a deeply drawn sigh and quite unconsciously in a stage whisper, "Poor Jonas!"

It was audible enough, however, to reach the object of her sympathy, who raised his head almost threateningly, but catching the sad expression of his sister's eye, the hopelessness of their twain cases and need for mutual sympathy, was suddenly revealed to him.

"Tabitha!" he whispered.

The real pathos of the situation for a moment nearly overcame its absurdity. There is little doubt that in another second the red curls of those heavily tried twin heads would have mingled alternately on breast and bosom, wet with a reciprocity of tears, wrung from hearts touched with the feeling of their own infirmities. Quite fortunately, perhaps, such an exhibition of Scrimp emotion was destined not to be, for at that crucial moment, unannounced, Lena, the "lady" assistant in the Scrimp kitchen, marched into the room and handed Jonas a letter, who, after one glance at its contents, hurriedly left the apartment, and lost to Tabitha, much to her chagrin, all opportunity of recounting her adventures at Seltzer's drug store, without her "button" and without her purse.

"Lena," said the mistress of Crocus cottage, "who was the letter for Mr. Jonas from?"

"Mr. Nigro, Miss."

"And who, for land's sake, is Mr. Nigro?"

"Why, you know him." said Lena, "Phil Nigro; some of them call him 'Dago Phil,' or 'Phil the Rustler'."

"And do you mean to tell me that you know Dago Phil, child?" said Miss Scrimp.

"Why, yes, Miss Tabitha," said the girl, now blushing consciously.

"Then," said Miss Scrimp, with a militant air, as she bore down upon the over-confiding Lena, "you must make up your mind between 'Dago Phil' and Crocus cottage; for that man's bad all through. I forbid him the house. Have a care, child, he means you no good!" and she reached for a gorgeous purple sun bonnet and stepped out into her garden patch, which was all aflame and fragrant with geraniums and asters, mignonette and sweet peas.

"Now is he?" asked Lena of herself reflectively, as she hesitated in the act of shaking the crumbs upon the carpet, "and he is so handsome and fair spoken. I think she's jealous of him, because he's so like Black Hereford." Then a sudden rush of recollection dyed her ruddy cheeks a deeper crimson, as the sensation caused by Phil's last night's kisses came back to her. "No, no," she whispered to herself, "Phil's all right, he'll be true to his — — — —."

"Le-na!" piped Miss Scrimp at this moment, in a frightened tremolo, from among the sweet peas, where she was maintaining a single-handed fight with a big bumblebee, and the girl, dropping both her reflections and the tablecloth, rushed outside to her mistress's assistance.

CHAPTER XIII

The Congress of the Cattle Kings.

Now, it must not be imagined for one instant that the mere fact of the existence of a lot of agitated breasts in Broncho County was going to interfere with the congress of the cattle kings. O, dear, no! for had the holding of the meeting been dependent upon the existence of hearts free from all emotional anxiety, none even of the chief promoters would have been present to take part in the debate, while the more prominent persons comprising the community would have been, as the "Jedge" would doubtless have remarked in the next issue of the Hustler, "conspicuous by their absence."

O, dear, no! hearts may bleed and break for that matter, as poor Miss Scrimp sobbingly admitted to herself in the privacy of her dimity draped chamber, but the "cold, unsympathetic world still wags cruelly on, callously exacting its sacrifice of the affections at the remorseless bugle call of duty." With which somewhat ambiguous and cheap platitude borrowed from what pulpit, she did not distinctly remember, Tabitha Scrimp put the finishing touches to a scarlet costume, in reckless disregard for the eternal fitness of things and in an ill-timed challenge to the known antipathies of the bovine race.

In accordance with the arrangements already made, Miss Scrimp, Sarza and the Cloverdale

party met in the ladies' parlor at the Bull's Head
the night of the congress, under the joint chape-
ronage of Mrs. Dean and Laban Hartland, the
latter of whom at the last moment, and after a
protracted search, had been found by Joe Parilla in
the granary, whither he had fled on assumed business, trusting to escape detection. Upon their
arrival at the town hall, though early upon the
scene, they found it already packed with a restless
throng, while the subdued murmur of hushed
voices filled the big assembly room. The arrival
of the Hartland party created an unusual commo-
tion, and necks were craned and heads were
turned, in more senses than one, of the cowboys
and their sweethearts, in order to catch a glimpse
of Phyllis and her sister, as they sailed up the
long aisle in advance of their father, to the seats
reserved for them.

They were dressed alike. Both had cream-
colored gowns of the same material, some light,
airy, cool looking fabric that clung to their figures
gracefully, and both wore very shady wide-brimmed
chip hats of the same color, artistically caught up
at the side and wreathed with broad bands of
purple violets.

On the platform were already collected the
leading cattlemen and farmers of the district, and
a few of the representative residents of Broncho
City. Most prominent among these were, of
course, Colonel Coboss, Dr. St. Lambert, Jim
Hereford, Jack Hardisty and Judge Quad, to the
first four of whom singular interest attached, on
account of the well known not altogether friendly
rivalry said to be existing between them, accent-

uated by hints of matters of the heart and other such things. The hall itself had been partially decorated for the occasion. The edges of the arch surrounding the stage were draped with looped lariats, intercepted at intervals with crossed stock whips and branding irons. A pyramid of graduated cheeses occupied one corner, and a churn resting upon a foundation of butter-tubs, the other. Above the center of the arch, the head of an enormous Texas bull, with tremendous sweep of horn, looked threateningly down upon the audience, its malevolent glass eyes almost hypnotizing Miss Scrimp in her scarlet tea-gown. Indeed, she was on the verge of hysterics, and would probably have fainted outright, had not Phyllis, with rare presence of mind, and amid the cheers of the audience, smothered her quaking little figure in her own snow-white mantle.

At last, Judge Quad stepped to the front of the platform and with a loud tap or two on one of the butter tubs, which sounded as hollow as a kettle-drum. but was the signal for a round of applause, called the meeting to order.

"Ladies and gentlemen of Broncho County and vicinity," he said, "on behalf of the committee who invited you to this meeting. I am delegated to ask you to select your chairman."

Then from all parts of the hall arose a tumult of voices and cries for "the mayor," "the Jedge," "Jonas Scrimp," and "Laban Hartland." When the voices ceased, the mayor rose from his seat in the audience, and in a short, business-like speech, suggested that "Mr. Laban Hartland, owing to his well known aversion to horned stock and hence his absolute impartiality as regarded the moot question of rival breeds of cattle, be requested to act as chairman." Greatly under protest, but amid the wildest cheering, Laban was conducted to the chair, while the editor of the Rustler was easily persuaded into acting as secretary.

Hartland was a ready speaker and when the necessity arose had the command of a most winning manner. His first words took the meeting by storm and placed him in thorough touch with every man, woman and child in the audience.

" Before we go any further," he said, " I want to know if there is any lady or gentleman among you who has managed to get into this hall without a 'button.' If there be, the penalty under the circumstances will be refreshments for the entire crowd. In this connection, I move that his honor, the mayor, and Mistress Tabitha Scrimp be a joint committee on credentials. I would also like to draw your attention to the fact, and in refutation of the mayor's contention that I have an aversion to horned stock, that I wear on the lappel of my coat not one, but *three* buttons, and I would like you to understand that I can see his honor's *one* solitary little button, and am ready to go him *two* better. How does that proposition strike you?"

The cowboys in the back seats yelled with delight.

" I would like to say that the fact of my wearing three buttons—which I understand when worn separately are intended to identify the wearer with either the Shorthorn, Jersey or Guernsey breed—will acquit me of any possible suspicion of partiality. I am equally impressed

with the inutility of all of them. Wheat's good
enough for me. If, however, you have any other
kind of 'button' to introduce, it will be my endeavor to see that its interests are duly protected."

He then went on to explain, as he understood
it, that the meeting was not called so much in the
interests of the cattleman as the dairyman; it was
not a question, he believed, of beef but of butter.
With due deference to the committee it seemed to
him that their invitation was misleading. It
might better have been addressed to the "Butter
Queens," many of whom, however, — God bless
them! — it was his privilege and his pleasure to
see were, by their presence tonight, helping to
push the good work along.

The gallantry of his remarks and his unpremeditated admission as to the "good work," fairly
brought down the house.

Phyllis waved her cream white hat until the
purple violets showered upon her bronze-brown
hair. The bull-punchers in the aisles pounded
upon the floor in their rowelled riding boots in
imitation of a stampede. Miss Scrimp, carried
away with the enthusiasm, bared her red shoulders
and shook Phyllis's white shawl aloft in hysterical
defiance of the stuffed bull; while Cornelius Kobb,
who was having a picnic all to himself in a remote
corner, hammered away with a big hickory stick
on the back of an unoccupied seat, and shouted
"B' Gosh!" and nothing else, as loud as he was
able.

When the uproar had subsided, Hartland endeavored to explain that it seemed to him that
his last words needed some qualifying, and amid

much laughter and cries of "No! no!" he managed to say that while he had no use for cows in the abstract, he was an epicure in the matter of good butter, and claimed he was no more seemingly inconsistent than his good friend, Colonel Coboss, who, though an enemy to the cultivation of wheat, always took mighty good care to have hot toast for breakfast, and whom as a most representative cattleman, he had now much pleasure in introducing to the audience.

When Laban resumed his seat he received an ovation.

When the master of Maverick rose to acknowledge the introduction, it was quite noticeable that though the applause that greeted him was to an extent liberal, it lacked spontaneity and seemed, as it were, local. A clapping of hands there, a rapping of sticks here, a stamping of feet in one place, led, as St. Lambert's quick eye noticed, by Dago Phil, and an occasional "hear, hear," from nowhere in particular. Had it been a case of pandemonium, he could not have received it with any greater show of outward approval. He was immaculately attired in dark trousers and a frock coat, which fitted his dragoon-like figure as a glove. His face, however, was as white as the big camelia on his breast, and wore a somewhat supercilious expression, but when he commenced to speak, he did so without the slightest trace of agitation.

"It seemed to him," he said, "that he was the last person who should have been called upon to address a gathering of dairymen. The objects of the meeting had, as Mr. Hartland stated, been somewhat misleading. He was a beefman first, last

and all the time. It was true, however, that since
Dr. St. Lambert had commenced experimenting
at the Cushla range with the object of discov-
ering, if he could, the best breed of dairy animals,
he had taken steps to experiment with some of his
own Shorthorns, with a view of ultimately ascer-
taining what class of animal in that particular
breed he ought to select, and also to discover the
secret of management that would lead to the best
results. Upon those lines he was now proceeding.
He considered it a waste of time to discuss the
question of superiority as between Jersey, Guernsey, and Shorthorn cows, as the latter animal was
conceded by all known authorities worth considering to be the queen of the dairy. A statement
that he would prove to the entire satisfaction of
Broncho County, whenever the representatives of
the — he would not say rival, but — competing
breeds met in an open test."

He took his seat.

It was as if a wet blanket studded with thistles
had been flung into the face of the meeting.

Dead silence prevailed for a few seconds after
Colonel Coboss finished speaking. When Hardisty
in a plainsman's deerskin coat, close fitting corded
hunting breeches and knee riding boots, picturesquely displaying his magnificent physique, stepped
to the front of the platform, he was held there for
a full minute with deafening applause. With his
deep sea gray eyes, he scanned the upturned faces
with brave and smiling composure.

"I'm sure you'll forgive me," he said, bowing
to the audience, "for addressing you unintroduced,
and you, sir," to the chairman, "for the intrusion,

for I am anticipating, I know, the order of the program. My name is Hardisty; I am herdsman on the Cushla Range. I merely wanted to say this: I believe the wishes of the audience would be better met, if in place of set speeches, we were to go in for short talks. Anyone who has anything to say let him speak right up in meeting and say it like a little man."

"That's what," and "You bet your sweet life," here came from different parts of the room.

"I am sure," he went on, "we may expect a lot of information from Colonel Coboss, if he will consent to forget he is not merely the master of Maverick, but a breeder of stock, upon the profitableness of which he depends for a living. Like the rest of us, he can, I'm sure, learn much by discussion. In order to set the ball rolling, I wish to insist, politely, but emphatically, that Col. Coboss is mistaken as to the Shorthorn being the greatest dairy animal, for, as regards quantity and quality of milk, cream, butter and cheese and cost of production, the Shorthorn is not in it with the Jersey cow. I have a dozen buttons on this hunting shirt," he added, "and they are all stamped in plain figures with a big 'J'."

"The impudence of the man," thought the Colonel; but his feelings were to receive a ruder shock, for when the uproar attending Hardisty's remarks had subsided, he said in a ringing voice, searching enough to have roused the coyote cubs on the Osage river, that he "would ask Colonel Coboss to display the button that represented the breed he championed."

Now, as great ill luck would have it, the master

of Maverick, after making his toilet, had completely forgotten to pick up one of the score or more Shorthorn buttons which were strewed on his dressing table.

"The deuce take it," he said to himself. "I'll stake my soul I've left that cursed little button behind."

The enormity of the offence seemed so over-whelming that he actually broke out in a cold perspiration, while Judge Quad buried his sallow face behind a milk can full of Miss Scrimp's sweet peas, that stood upon the table. It flashed upon him that he had been placed in an absurd and humiliating position, and worse than all, in the presence again of Phyllis Hartland. Premeditated perhaps, and all through that conceited ass, Hardisty. The gray ash color overspread the pupils of his eyes. He would teach the fellow a lesson. No, not now, he would bide his time, but he turned a look of ill disguised hatred upon the tawny bearded man who encountered his glance with an expression of the coldest good humor. Hardly able to articulate, he stepped over to Laban Hartland, with whom he whispered excitedly for a moment.

"Colonel Coboss has asked me to explain," said Hartland, "that the omission, as we all know, is purely accidental, but that he is prepared to pay the penalty, and has offered, with the approval of the meeting, and I might say with great liberality, to place the forfeit in the shape of a five hundred dollar cash prize to be presented to the owner of the winning cow, in the first public competition that takes place between a Shorthorn and a Jersey cow in Broncho County."

Then ear-splitting whoops and cheers, and cries of "Coboss!" "Hardisty!" "Shorthorn!" and "Jersey!" made the town hall shake in a way, so said the "Jedge," as it had not done since he presided at the last political convention. But further demonstrations were yet to follow. Coboss's insolent glance had aroused in Hardisty a determination to "rub it in," which conclusion was rendered final by an unmistakably contemptuous stare, with which Black Jim also continued steadily to regard him.

"It is now in order for me," he said, "to point out another delinquent member," and he indicated Hereford. "Colonel Coboss's chief ranger has, like his good master, also forgotten to display his credentials. May I ask Mr. Hereford to show up his button?"

Hereford sprang to his feet shaking with suppressed anger, and it is hard to say what the consequences might not have been, for he was advancing toward Hardisty in an almost menacing way, when Laban Hartland with surprising presence of mind, smilingly intercepted him.

"I am authorized by Mr. Hereford," he said a moment later, "to tell you that he also admits his buttonless condition, and, in evidence of his contrition, he has explained to me his willingness to donate fifty dollars for the same purpose, on precisely the same conditions, as the prize offered by Colonel Coboss.

Again the invisible rafters rang with the shouts of the cow-punchers; the meeting was yelling itself hoarse. Miss Tabitha Scrimp, of course hysterically overcome this time with what she considered

Mr. Hereford's " sweet magnanimity," once more bared her narrow red shoulders and shook her scarlet mittened hands full in the face of the Texas bull, whose angry glass eyes seemed to roll in their putty sockets, as they reflected the crimson of her frock.

When the shouting had ceased, the mayor rose from the body of the hall and addressing the chair said that " he had been requested by a rural friend to insist — and he knew that his deeply interested colleague on credentials, Miss Scrimp, would sustain the point — to insist that the two buttonless members on the platform should supply themselves with the proper badge of qualification forthwith."

Laughter loud and long followed this sally, while the two persons chiefly interested looked not only daggers but deringers, to boot. Then, when after a moment's hesitation, Phyllis Hartland, with rare exhibition of womanly tact, and with a grace and bravery that won every heart in the audience, stood up and asked to be permitted " to supply the forgotten buttons, " Broncho County as represented in the town hall simply went mad, stark, raving, hopelessly mad. But, when a moment later she mounted the platform, and, after courtesying to the audience in her own irresistible way, pinned the missing buttons, which had caused so much ado, on the respective coats of Colonel Coboss and Black Hereford, whose pale faces were a study of alternating humility, exaltation, admiration and defiance, the house lost control of itself, stampeded, and for the next five minutes, the building bent before a vocal tornado.

But, though the time was getting on and no

business so far accomplished, the crowd was blind
to Hartland's gesticulations for order, and when at
last comparative peace was almost restored, the
tumult was again precipitated by Cornelius Kobb,
who, in a corner by himself, after hammering away
with his hickory stick like a demon, was overheard
to remark, evidently intended only for his own
ears, "Y'ere right, Cornelius, b'gosh that gal o'
Hartland's out o' sight!"

When Hartland was at last heard, he said he
was sorry to say that Dr. St. Lambert, who was to
have said something in reference to both Guernseys and Jerseys, on which, as they knew, he was
experimenting, was called away suddenly on a
mission of professional mercy. Colonel Coboss
and Mr. Hereford had both asked to be excused
from speaking, and Judge Quad, though he was
always ready to throw open the columns of the
Rustler and air the opinions of others, was not in a
position to discuss dairy matters, having devoted
all his attention to beef cattle. As for himself, as
they knew, he — well he might as well say it to
ease his own mind, and assure them no offence
was intended — he had personally no use for the
prong-horned devils — and Tabitha exchanged
glances with the Texas bull and the crowd cheered
ironically — "but he was more than glad to be of
any service to them. Would they express their
wishes?"

CHAPTER XIV

Jack Hardisty Points Out the Milky Way.

Laban Hartland had not long to wait for an expression of the wishes of the audience, for immediately there arose calls for " Hardisty," " Jersey Jack," " Jack, the Broncho buster," the " Jack o' Trumps " and so on, and then a consultation between the herdsman and the chairman, when the latter stated that he " had requested Mr. Hardisty to say a few words, and asked their kind indulgence."

Then Hardisty, who after addressing his hearers as " Butter Queens and Cattle Kings," and assuring the chairman that nothing personal was intended in his forthcoming references, commenced his remarks by insisting that " the time had arrived for the farmers — of whom there were nearly four millions seven hundred thousand families in America — to materially reduce the acreage they now devoted to the cultivation of wheat."

" Unless the farmer," he said, " wants to sink hopelessly in the mire, he must discount the present enormous production, so that the national crop, outside the demands of home consumption, will not exceed the normal requirements of the export trade. The average yearly consumption of wheat, he said, in the United States, was a little less than five bushels for every man, woman and child in the land, and yet forsooth, we raised a crop of six hundred million bushels of wheat every

twelvemonth.   Little wonder that it was only
fifty cents a bushel in Chicago, or that nearly thirty
per cent of the farmers had mortgages on their
property.   Why, the crop in many states cost almost twice as much to harvest, as its sale netted to
the unfortunate farmer, who in the matter of raising wheat was competing with the serf labor of the
Old World."   And he turned from the audience
to glance at Laban Hartland, who moved uneasily
in his chair.   "He was glad to think, however,
that the Iowa grangers were not wholly blind to
their interests, for the acreage sown to wheat today
was nearly two millions and a half less than in the
preceding year.   It may have been all right in
1880," he said, "when wheat was a dollar, but
now the agriculturist must look for another outlet
for his labor; he would have to take to mixed
farming and stock, and dairy stock at that.   Was
he right?"

And Cornelius Kobb thrashed the furniture
with his hickory stick, and the farmers cheered
to the echo.

Hardisty continued.   "When I say dairy
stock, I mean it, for the latest official returns show
by the falling off in the number of cattle, one
million seven hundred thousand head last year,
that the great ranch kings have found it necessary,
on account of the decline in the price of beef, to
draw in their horns." and he threw a quizzical
glance at Colonel Coboss.   "But I also find, sir,"
he said, addressing Hartland, "that the number of
milch cows is rapidly on the increase, and individ-
ually growing in value.   I find sir," he went on,
—oblivious of, or ignoring, the fact that the

chairman scorned the "horned devils" — "and I know it will also interest you to hear, that while the average value of a milch cow in Iowa is only about twenty-one dollars, in the state of Massachusetts, where the breeding of the dairy animal has reached the highest state of perfection, and where providence also seems to take special pains in producing the most perfect specimens of the human race," — and he inclined his head toward the front benches and bowed to Hartland, who laughingly acknowledged the compliment, while the audience rose to its feet and cheered, — "I find, sir, that the average price in Massachusetts is thirty-two dollars, eleven dollars more than the average value in the state of Iowa; and I further find, sir, that seventy-five per cent. of these animals are Jerseys!"

The hickory stick thrashed louder than ever, and fully two-thirds of the meeting waved their hats and yelled like savages.

"Comment," he went on to say, "seems unnecessary; but when we remember that out of the sixteen million milch cows in the United States, Iowa owns one million three hundred thousand, it would be also well for us to remember that if seventy-five per cent. of them were Jerseys, as is the case in Massachusetts, instead of being worth only twenty-seven million dollars, they might be worth forty-one million six hundred thousand dollars! In the face of these facts, sir, I ask whether it is not worth our while, not only to prosecute dairy farming more vigorously, but to select the most profitable breed of animals. Land, except in the extreme northwestern states, is get-

ting too valuable for the mere grazing of cattle
and production of beef. Both beef and grain are
steadily decreasing in value, while the value of
first class milk and butter is constantly on the increase." He then gave some facts and figures in
proof of his argument which he challenged anyone
to refute, and closed his reference to dairy
products by asking "if ordinary milk, which in
the large cities is worth five cents a quart, and
Jersey milk eight cents, and good ordinary butter
twenty-five cents and Jersey butter forty cents,
was n't it time for the farmer, in selecting animals
for his dairy, to have a single eye for their butter
qualifications and not for their beef?"

"One more vitally important factor," he said,
" had to be considered in the profitable handling
of dairy stock, and that was the question of fodder, for upon that was largely dependent the
value of the product of the cow. It was impossible to exaggerate the importance to the
human family of pure milk," and he appealed to
the mothers present, and here, Miss Scrimp
assumed a maternal air. He also regretted that
Dr. St. Lambert had been called away, who had
intended to give them the results of his own investigation. He also wanted to emphasize the feasi-
bility, if circumstances demanded it, of storing
silage as the Egyptians did their grain, so that in
years of plenty they could provide against seasons
of drouth.

"We preserve and can our fruit and meat for
ourselves," he said, "and why not hermetically
seal and preserve in air-tight chambers our corn,
our silage and our fodder? Products so treated

while in their naturally moist state, will retain
their normal condition for an indefinite period and
lose none of their virtues.   Through the instrumentality of first class fodder, and first class cows,
mixed farming and rotation of crops, the farmer
would at last be entering upon days of pleasant-
ness and paths of peace.

"Up to the present time, the farmer who had
devoted his exclusive attention to the production
of staple cereals only, had been completely at the
mercy of the mercenary middle-man and of the
trusts.   While the farmer had been farming his
land by the sweat of his brow, the combines, as a
matter of fact, by another sweating process, of a
more far-reaching character, had been farming the
hoodwinked farmer.   He was at the mercy of a
well drilled army of commercial regulators.   These
were facts!   Of the total amount of the annual
national exports, the farmer contributed as his
share, by his superhuman efforts and a chronic
backache, seventy-eight per cent.

"I would like to know," he asked, "what
percentage of profit on this enormous sum, which
has amounted to nearly eight hundred million
dollars every year, has found its way into the
pockets of the farmers. Perhaps the chairman,
who raised wheat at a cost of ten or more dollars
an acre, and sold it at six dollars or less, could
tell the meeting.

"My friends," he said. drawing close to the
edge of the platform and inciting the admiration
of every one, Phyllis Hartland included, by the
personality of his magnificent presence, and the
resonance of his voice, "you, who as the princes

of labor, are the true backbone of this great country, see to it that you are no longer used as the football for monopolists, or the shuttlecocks of your own self-will. I know a path that is open to you, extending an invitation, whose profitable portal, if you will but enter it and then explore, will assuredly lead you to both competence and happiness. It will also relieve you of the perpetual drudgery of the plowshare and the harrow, and the embarrassing visits of the persistent collector. For want of a better name, I have called it 'the Milky Way.' It is not hard to find. A Jersey cow is the sign post. Will you follow it?"

If the former plaudits of the meeting could rightly have been likened to a vocal tornado, that which followed Hardisty's speech may well be characterized as a cyclone. The enthusiastic confusion that ensued was a fair imitation of an earthquake. The cowboys smote each other on their buckskin coats with their heavy, open palms, and an energy that resembled the pounding of tough beefsteaks. Spurs jingled, stock whips cracked, the small boys in large quantities yelled their rhyming alphabetical belief in the Jersey cow, and the veteran hayseeds from the crossroads stowed their chews temporarily and joined in the tumult. Lovers took advantage of the uproar and stole without remonstrance extra squeezes that were not on the programme. Even the mothers were carried away, forgot home cares, and shouted their soprano admiration, while the babies, staunch converts to the principles enunciated by Hardisty, sought to drown their fears in deep drawn draughts of maternal milk.

After Hardisty had taken his seat, a show of hands was called for, not, as the chairman declared, to pass upon the merits of the three breeds, as no comparative proof had been submitted, but in order to show the relative strength of the various sympathizers present.

The Guernsey men were first called upon, when about one-fourth of the audience stood up; then the Shorthorn men were asked to commit themselves, and fully a third of the meeting rose and cheered, the master of Maverick and Black Hereford both coming to the front of the platform and joining in the demonstration, and which latter act well-nigh precipitated a riot between the factions, for the mayor rose and said that he and others present would like to be " informed as to the denomination of the buttons worn by the Colonel and his friend."

Laban Hartland explained to the meeting that they were " Jersey" buttons, and here his voice was drowned in the cheers and counter cheers that followed.

Then Cicero Brief, the argumentative county attorney, spoke up and laughingly called attention to the fact that the action of the leaders of the Shorthorn party had proved they were false to their colors, whichever way they liked to look at it. They had no right to vote for Shorthorns and wear Jersey buttons, whilst if they voted for the Jerseys, they must needs swallow their principles, for they could not of course as gentlemen contemplate discarding their badges, considering the source from whence they obtained them.

Cries of " Oh! Oh! " followed this, also some

remarks not entirely flattering to the lawyer and then there was a sudden lull in the hurly-burly, merely the lull before the storm. And this would inevitably have burst had not Phyllis Hartland, who had been following the course of events with many misgivings and a beating heart, suddenly arisen and in her most gracious way begged that neither Colonel Coboss nor Mr. Hereford would dream of allowing themselves to be placed in a false position, merely because she was an innocent accessory to the crime. " Would they not please throw the unfortunate little buttons away, or exchange them for two Miss Scrimp had of a less objectionable stripe, and release themselves from the horns of the dilemma."

It was then that Colonel Coboss saw an opportunity, as he thought, to rehabilitate himself in the eyes of Phyllis Hartland.

" No," he said, " not for a moment would either Mr. Hereford or himself contemplate surrendering a souvenir so highly prized, neither did he seek or need lessons in courtesy from so faulty an exponent of manners as the person who had last spoken. As for himself and the Jersey button he had the honor of wearing, he should treasure it for all time, not on account of the letter it bore but as an evidence of the exalted estimation in which he held its fair donor. He begged to propose three cheers for the Jerseys and their distinguished advocate, Miss Phyllis Hartland."

Then the congress of cattle kings became a matter of history.

CHAPTER XV

Sizing Up the Situation.

There is little doubt but that the congress of the cattle kings—an account of which with numerous embellishments, entirely filled the columns of the next issue of the Rustler—presented to the citizens of Broncho an admirable opportunity for reaching a just estimate of the chief participators in the events of that evening. An estimate, however, which placed the various individuals in an entirely different light to that in which many of them had previously been regarded by the public.

From now on, an added interest centered in those persons who had been more or less prominent at that celebrated gathering. While opinions differed greatly as to the quality of the attributes to be accorded in most instances, no difference of opinion, expressed or unexpressed, existed in regard to a prominent few. Laban Hartland had appeared in an altogether new light, and the entire community, with a few notable exceptions, had come out strong in their expressions of goodwill and sympathy for a man they had hitherto been relentless in condemning. While still regarding with complete disfavor his wilful loyalty to wheat, they had seen so much in the man of affability, shrewdness and humor to admire, that their former sense of contempt for his stubborn ways was now converted into a strong feeling of compassion for his persistent perversity. This was coupled with an honest desire to extend the right hand of practical sympathy if the need should arise.

Cornelius Kobb voiced the sentiment of the Osage valley. "Old man Hartland's all right. Ef he quits wheat, we'll send him to Congress."

As for Jack Hardisty, he awoke the next day to find himself famous. His looks, his deferential courtesy and his resonant voice had taken the hearts of all the women by storm, while his "horse sense" and magnificent coolness and nerve under the fire of Col. Coboss and Hereford's malignant gaze, was not lost upon the cowpunchers. They were already wagering piebald pintos and flea-bitten cayuses against plugs of nigger-head on the result of a not improbable encounter between Black Jim Hereford and the handsome herdsman from the Cushla ranch. With the dairymen and farmers he was the hero of the hour; his wide knowledge and sensible grasp of a subject so closely related to their profession and their pockets, having wholly conquered them.

In the matter of the master of Maverick and his chief ranger, however, much diversity of opinion existed. By a large wing of the "broncho-busting" fraternity, headed by Dago Phil, the Colonel himself was well advertised as the most liberal man in the district, and the only real gentleman at the congress of the cattle kings, St. Lambert, perhaps, excepted.

Whoever called him a "chump" was a "rufous liar," according to Dago Phil, and one he would no more hesitate to bore full of air holes than he would a gopher. It should be mentioned that a lavish circulation of the Colonel's currency

was in part responsible for this display of chivalry.
There is little doubt that the Colonel's liberal
donation, quite unpremeditated, it is true, (but
why go behind things?) and his somewhat effusive
gallantry at the close of the meeting, resented by
more than one person present, had, as he had fully
calculated, mitigated, if it had not altogether
removed, the ridiculous impression the button incident had made upon the meeting. He had offered
a very handsome prize, and had further extricated
himself out of a deucedly humiliating position, by
adopting with an unnecessary amount of flam,
perhaps, the only course open to any gentleman
under the circumstances. He had voted for a rival
breed of cattle, that was magnanimity, and he had
played upon the feelings of both pit and gallery
when he had suggested the unusual course of
cheering a lady, but in this instance the most
popular woman in the county. Taking it all in all,
he had, perhaps, gained more friends than he had
lost, a condition of things that was duly and from
time to time reported to him by his unprincipled
henchman, and over which fact he warmly con-
gratulated himself, realizing that the greater his
popularity, the greater chance existed for the
ultimate attainment of his heart's desire—the winning of Phillis Hartland.

With James Hereford, the state of affairs was,
if anything, reversed. His silence on the platform
in the face of his pantomimic actions, led to the
unfair belief that he was actuated by fear, whereas
his silence was entirely due to the fact that his
temper was beyond control. He had felt that any
attempt at speech would have resulted in his own

committal. The false construction that had been
placed upon his motives by the many, were not,
however, shared by a limited few, principally
women, who with feminine intuition, had read
between the lines and seen the pitiful demon of
jealousy dominating over all. Neither of these
views, however, was adopted by Miss Scrimp.
While she fully believed that Mr. Hereford was a
victim to a tempest of the heart, she concluded,
greatly to her maidenly satisfaction, as she gazed
upon her own crimson reproduction in the mirror,
that the cause of the dear fellow's utter embarass-
ment was not far to seek. And she let fall the
sparse glory of her red ringlets and hummed in
discreet falsetto,

"O, why hast thou taught me to love thee?
O, why hast thou taught this fond bosom to sigh?"
while she coyly rolled her curl papers and prepared
to retire.

Among the fraternity of the lariat, however,
Hereford had further forfeited the waning estimation in which he was held.

If Hartland had gained so in public estimation,
what of his daughter?

It is no exaggeration to say, after the incidents
that followed so fast upon each other's heels, the
night of the demonstration, at the town hall, that
Phyllis Hartland was the most overwhelmingly
popular person, man or woman, in all the country
side. Not only was there not a man in Broncho
City or on a ranch or farm, who would not have
considered it an especial mark of honor to
be called upon to do her the most trivial service,
but the women themselves were violently in love

with her. She was by their grace, the handsomest,
most industrious, noblest, least conceited, smartest,
best daughter, and — yes, this was also admitted —
the "best dressed woman they had ever seen, God
bless her!" and this with a sincerity there was no
mistaking. No wonder the men were crazy about
her. It required no search warrant to disclose the
fact.

Upon this they all agreed over an afternoon
cup of Ceylon tea at Crocus Cottage, where, at
Miss Scrimp's invitation, they had met to talk
over the events of that memorable evening. "It
did not require a telescope to see that Colonel
Coboss, my dear, was hopelessly infatuated," said
one. Nor that "handsome Jack Hardisty was
forever looking her way, whenever there was the
least shadow of an excuse," said another. "As
for Black Hereford," said a third, "he almost
devoured her at times with those jet eyes of his."
While a fourth said that she had heard "that
Hereford had actually formally asked her hand of
the old gentleman."

It was this announcement that was responsible
for an article in next week's Rustler under the
head of "Society Snap Shots" wherein it was
stated that "the injury to Miss Scrimp's, well —
ankle, was not as serious as at first reported, but
that the Maltese cat was dead!"

The alleged unfaithfulness of the black herdsman had brought such a rush of tears to the poor
soul's eyes that in reaching for the cake basket to
hide her confusion, she had brought the pointed
toe of her toothpick boot into violent contact with
the unprotected back of her favorite kitten.

While many such compliments and criticisms as these, and more of a similar nature, were being circulated to Phyllis Hartland's infinite credit, and which, according to all established superstition, should have made that young lady's ears burn furiously — she, entirely unconcious of the spirit of admiration she had excited, continued heroically to perform her self-allotted round of daily drudgery. This she had with complete surrender of her own comfort and inclination imposed upon herself. The future had to be faced — a future, thanks to her poor father's blind infatuation in the matter of wheat, and groundless opposition to mixed farming, dairying or stock, held out but little hope of financial betterment. It is true, she reflected, that he had conceded a point — a concession fraught with all manner of future possibilities — but as it was only a concession extracted by her feminine diplomacy, and through no sense of conviction on his part, the value of the victory could not be rated very highly.

Anyway, there were two cows at last installed in the home paddock, and while some butter had still to be purchased, no money, (thank heaven!) had to be outlayed on milk. The Plymouth Rocks and the Spangled Hamburghs proved fully worthy of Mrs. Cornelius Kobb's high recommendation, who assured Phyllis that she could " positively rely upon their strict attention to business." Had it not " taken her old man most of his time just a collectin' the hen fruit." But as a large proportion of the products of both the cows and the hens were consumed upon the premises, for which, though she was given due credit, she received no

money, she had to depend upon other sources to re-
quite her time and enterprise in cash. The Berkshire
pigs were thriving, but while she expected much
from them in the future, she could look for no returns as yet. By spring, perhaps, she might hope to
realize on the investment.

While she, with Ruth's assistance, was thus
devoting her mornings to gaining an insight
into the mysteries of the dairy and the infantile
ailments of her chicks and the proper feed for
poultry and pigs, questions and occasions arose
when a man's advice and assistance were absolutely necessary. So it came about in the most
natural way that Dr. St. Lambert, who was only
too ready for any excuse that would throw him
into Ruth's society, would drive over to Cloverdale at least once during the week. Nor was it
surprising that Jack Hardisty, who was an expert
on matters relating to all kinds of farm stock,
should frequently accompany him. And so it came
about that thrown so constantly into each other's
society, and dependent as was Phyllis in her own
case upon Hardisty's advice in such trivial matters
as "pip" and "silage," which was always reliable,
she sought the opinion of the tawny bearded ranch-
man on more important matters affecting Cloverdale and her father's strange administration of the
farm. Neither does it seem more unnatural —
indeed, how could it have failed to be otherwise?—
that before long, Hardisty should have secretly
surrendered himself body and soul to Phyllis Hartland's irresistible and conquering ways.

But Phyllis had other matters besides cocks
and hens and round-bodied pigs to tax her time

and attention. Miss Scrimp and Lena with their
lessons in deportment, singing and music, were
two least important of the pupils on her list.
Not only in Broncho City, but at many a neighboring ranch and prosperous farm house, the
occasion of her visits of tuition were regarded as
red-letter days. Had she been a duchess, she
could not have been treated with greater consideration. The best the house could offer was never
considered good enough for her. She had a way
with her, too, without any encouragement on her
own part, that prompted young and old of both
sexes to impart to her their most sacred confidences
and unlock the chambers of their hearts. She,
being strongly impressed with the necessity for
method and the strict observance of business
obligations, never permitted storm or shine to
interfere with her roll-call of duty. So that the
picture of a superb looking woman in a dark-
green habit, with ash-colored sombrero and
hawk's wing, mounted on a big slashing sorrel
mare galloping over the dusty prairie trail or
threading the dripping bridle-paths through the
thickets, soon came to be recognized by cowboy
and granger as being quite as reliable for the purpose of fixing a date as almanac or calendar.

It was upon the emoluments derived from this
disposition of her time, together with her salary
as organist of the township church, and the work
of her artistic needle, that Phyllis had relied for the
present to look for the furtherance of the object
she had in view.

September had come and gone. The harvest,
if such it could be called, with its tribute of

stunted straw and undeveloped heads of wheat, had been garnered, and Laban Hartland's granary, now moss-grown from disuse, was not much less empty than his pocket. On the tenth of the month, Jonas Scrimp together with Dago Phil, who of late it had been noticed was often to be seen in the company of the fussy little attorney, and to whom Phyllis had taken an intuitive aversion, had called for the half yearly instalment on the mortgage, due at noon of that day.

It was Saturday, Phyllis's " off day," as she expressed it. No singing, no music, no physical culture, excepting that of " home development." With a saucy looking housemaid's cap perched upon the masses of her bronze brown hair, and the sleeves of a very pale blue tightly fitting print gown well rolled up, revealing the soft roundness of her bare, white arms, she was illustrating to Sarza, during the intervals of stirring up some flour in a big bake pan, some of her favorite calisthenic attitudes, when the shadows of two men darkened the kitchen doorway.

" Morning, Mr. Scrimp," she said in her airiest manner, "' won't you step in?"

He would, but then catching a peep of Sarza, he muttered something about the hall door and Mr. Hartland, and bolted.

Laban had a cheque already filled out for the amount, much to Jonas's amazement. In calculating the interest he was a dollar or two astray in his figures. The difference was insisted upon.

" I won't call you a mortgage shark, Mr. Scrimp," said he in his hearty way, " but you attorneys are perfect Shylocks when it's a case of

compound interest. I haven't the right change.
You cannot make it, eh? Perhaps your man,"
turning to Dago Phil, "will ask my daughter
if she can break five dollars," and he handed him
a bank bill.

Upon receipt of her father's message, Phyllis
hastened to her own den, as she called it, a room
added to the original house at her own special request, where she wrote, read, posted her farm
accounts, thought, played the mandolin and entertained a select few of her chosen friends. Upon
locking her secretary, after taking out the change
required, and turning around, she was as much
annoyed as surprised to see Dago Phil standing at
the doorway.

"You are intruding," she said.

"Pardon, Miss," he replied, "I thought I was
told to follow you," (and if truth be told, he was)
"and besides, Lena, the girl, you know, who works
for Miss Scrimp, has told me of the strange motto
in your parlor and I — I wanted to read it."

On the wall opposite, painted in big old-English
capitals on a piece of French-gray cardboard,
which was kept in place by some tiny rosettes of
black and gold ribbon, was the following quota-
tion from George Herbert —

> "A servant with this clause
> Makes drudgery divine!
> Who sweeps a room as to Thy laws,
> Makes it and th' action fine."

"Indeed!" said Phyllis very coldly, and locking the door behind her with the air of a turnkey,
"I hope then you'll carry home that moral to Lena,
that is, if you are quite sure you understand it."

CHAPTER XVI

Fire! Fire! Fire!

It was the evening of March the 9th, six months, all but one day, since the events as narrated in the preceding chapter, and Phyllis, mounted on her big sorrel mare, was splashing her way through pools of melted snow that dotted the yielding, desolate prairie on her way to an Easter choir practice at the cross-road church. Allowing her horse to pick its own path between yellow snowdrifts and black puddles, she cast a mental retrospect of the events that had transpired during the last half year, now on the eve of expiration.

Yes, it was full of food for reflection. The winter had been a typical one from a climatic standpoint — pronounced even for Iowa. Furious snow storms had in a measure retrieved the character of the heavens, and condoned in a way for the summer's awful drougth. The land no longer creaked with thirst; it babbled with water. Magnificent sleighing had encouraged winter gaieties. Dances and other entertainments had brightened the long evenings, and an all round extension of social amenities had drawn most of those persons with whom the reader is now fairly well familiar, into closer bonds of intimacy, and in some instances into much nearer and dearer relations. While

Ruth had become engaged to Maryann St. Lambert, Phyllis still remained — so far as could be seen — heart whole and fancy free. In this respect her friends declared her to be inscrutable. As much, however, could scarcely be said of either Coboss or Hereford, whose manifestations of the love that consumed them, though concealed from each other, was now an open secret to the rest of the world. As for Hardisty, though the drift of his aspirations was suspected, he guarded his own affairs with a manly dignity that resisted every wile of the impertinent tormentor.

Among other diversions there had of course been an entertainment at Broncho City town hall. This was for the benefit of the Crippled Cowboy's Union. Here it was that Phyllis, being a young woman who fully appreciated all the gifts of the Gods — beauty included — had robed herself in a ravishing gown of the palest blue and with a cluster of big golden chrysanthemums at her corsage and in the folds of her pretty hair, had danced and sung herself into the hearts of the entire audience. With St. Lambert and Hardisty as tenor and baritone, Ruth's soprano and her own glorious contralto, they had given a rendition of

"O, who will o'er the downs so free"

that had literally, as Judge Quad of course remarked in the columns of his paper, "broken up the house."

It was on this occasion likewise that Miss Scrimp was also presented with an opportunity — long dreamed of — of "bringing down the house." With Jim Hereford at her elbow to turn over the pages of her music, she sang with such a refreshing disregard for the stuffed Texas bull, time and tune, as to fairly electrify her auditors and cover Hereford with confusion.

"O, why hast thou taught me to love thee?
O, why has thou taught this fond bosom to sigh?"
and she looked from the keyboard into Hereford's face —
"O, why does thy presence thus move me?
Why flushed is my cheek and why languid my eye?"
and then she turned with a visible moisture between its lids that much afflicted and slightly squinting member full upon the audience. At the bare recollection of all of which, a smile spread over Phyllis's face and she burst out laughing.

But if there had been a liberal leaven of fun and rural dissipation, there had also been much to tax her patience and resolution. Though with all the troubles and anxieties — and a glow of excusable self-satisfaction here possessed her — there was indeed much to be thankful for. It was only today that her father had reminded her — goodness knows there was little need — that tomorrow another half yearly payment on the mortgage fell due, and admited with tears dangerously close to the surface, that unless money came from some unexpected quarter, ejectment from Cloverdale would inevitably result, as Colonel Coboss had declared through Jonas Scrimp that prompt foreclosure would follow non-payment. He had not, however, told Phyllis that sorely trying to his own dignity he had actually pleaded with the master of Maverick for a brief extension of time, or how that upon one condition only, the latter had declared his willingness to accede.

"Exercise judiciously your paternal rights," he had written to Laban, "and support my suit for your daughter's hand and I will grant you all the time you desire."

Neither did he dare tell her of his indignant refusal, or how that he replied "his daughter was the sole mistress of her own heart, and that the man who hoped to win her need expect neither support nor opposition from him. He could proceed as he saw fit."

But he did tell her of Joe Parilla's generous offer of his savings and how he had firmly though kindly rejected it. But what *was* he to do? Could his brave daughter with her fund of resources suggest any expedient, and loop-hole of escape?

Then Phyllis glowed again with honest pride as she remembered how that she had answered, "Yes, daddy dear, God and Phyllis will come to the rescue "—which, to put it mildly, was an original way of describing her co-operative plan for his financial salvation.

And she further remembered how she had led him to her "den" and showed him greatly to his amazement her savings-bank book, wherein was posted to her infinite but very personal credit, various sums which totalled in the aggregate an amount slightly in excess of that which was needed to meet Colonel Coboss's implacable demand, and how she had listened to his phrases of gratitude and vehement expressions of praise. And as she rode into the driving shed of the little meeting-house, she could see in her mind's eye snugly secreted in the small brass-bound cash box in her secretary, the fat roll of bills that was destined to allay her father's fears and stay Jonas Scrimp's exacting greed for another six months.

When at last she was seated at the organ and, while waiting for the arrival of the choristers, was flooding the small building with the full rich melody of tremolo and diapason, she was conscious of the presence of a spectator, and looking suddenly up for an instant, on the outside saw Dago Phil's pale, evil face pressed against the window. The next moment the arrival of the choir drove the incident from her mind.

The practice was a long one. The Easter hymn she had selected,

"Jesus Christ has risen today,"

with its chorus of hallelujahs, demanded persistent rehearsing and by the time she had succeeded in instilling the necessary amount of triumphant harmony into its rendition and had dismissed her little band of rosy cheeked minstrels, put away her music and locked the church door, the new moon was no longer visible.

The sorrel mare welcomed her with a whimper, and thrust its cold, velvety nose against her face. A moment later she was in the saddle, and urging Starlight into a sharp canter, struck across the reeking prairie for Cloverdale and comfort.

She headed for the distant bluff where somewhat to her confusion, she had been intercepted by Hereford last summer, but gave it a wider berth than usual, preferring for some undefined reason the open plain, and gave free license to Starlight and her own reflections.

"Tomorrow! Ah, yes, tomorrow! God *was* so good and life was *so* sweet, after all. What a sur-

prise it had been to her dear, dear father, and what
a surprise it would be tomorrow, to crafty old
Jonas Scrimp, and what confusion to all his plans,
and more than likely also to that sinister confederate
of his, Dago Phil ; " and inwardly constrained at this
moment to look up, a small patch of lurid glow on
the horizon arrested and riveted her attention.

" What could it be?   Not the rising moon,
surely.   And yet momentarily it seemed to grow
in bulk, and mount higher.   No, it could not be
the moon, she was foolish ; the idea of a full moon
rising in the west at this time of night.   If not the
moon, then what was it? Yes, what was it? Why,
it was in a direct line with Cloverdale, and as she
drew nearer to it, it increased, yes, surely increased
in brilliancy and in size.   And now shafts and
tongues of light seemed to leap upwards and the
sky above grew red and threatening.   Why, it
must be fire!

" What did she say? Fire? "

Aye, fire! fire! fire!

" Oh, Starlight," she sobbed, " Cloverdale is on
fire.   May God have mercy on us ! "

And in answer to poor Phyllis's unuttered appeal, the brave beast broke into a furious gallop
and bore his weeping mistress towards their burning home.

CHAPTER XVII

Checkmate.

When Phyllis Hartland reached Cloverdale ten minutes later, bespattered with mud and foam, she found that though the fire had not as yet attacked the bungalow itself, the annex wherein was located her den and bed room, was a mass of charred rafters and glowing coals, while flames now fanned by a rapidly increasing wind, were leaping along the short connecting corridor and threatening the main building.

On the driveway by the piazza, without hat or coat, frantically gesticulating and in apparent argument with Joe Parilla and a stableman, stood her father, the picture of abject despair. As she approached the group, Laban flew to her side and in excited tones proceeded to relate the story of the disaster.

"Please not now," she interrupted later on, "but tell me at once if my cash box and the papers were saved?"

"The cash box! Yes," he replied, "we found it open and the bankbook gone, but that is nothing, dearie, the bank will —"

"Nothing,"! she interrupted. "Why, father." she went on, "don't you understand? The money to meet the mortgage was in the box. I drew the cash from the bank yesterday and placed it there for safe keeping until tomorrow.

My God!" she continued, "it's almost tomorrow now."

For a moment she bowed her head in her hands, while Laban, wholly overcome, staggered towards the porch, where Mrs. Dean, as white as a ghost in the fitful glare, stood with Ruth and Roxie trembling at her side, and soothing Daisy's fears upon her bosom.

The crackling flames aroused Phyllis. Beckoning to Joe Parilla and the stableman, she flew rather than ran across the yard to the carriage shed, from which in a few moments they all three emerged dragging a long coil of canvas-covered hose behind them. This, in obedience to her instructions, while they yet marvelled what possible scheme she had in view, they now connected with the great pump beneath the windmill, and then her purpose gradually dawned upon them.

"Tony," she said, "draw the slack of the hose as close to the fire as you dare; and you, Joe, see that the connecting rod is secure, then throw the mill into gear and let's all pray for wind."

But they had little need for prayer in this particular, their wishes were anticipated. For a moment the great mill that had stood so long idle seemed to resent the imposition of honest labor; but as the big sails swung into the face of the cold east wind, that seemed to gather strength as it realized the full significance of the new demand upon its might, they yielded to its command, and after a moment's trembling and creaking resistance, were whirled into activity.

An abundance of water, a two-inch nozzle, and a well directed battery under Phyllis's personal direction, soon did the rest; the further progress of the fire was checked. But there was nothing to show for the loss of her cherished rooms, her books, her music and her hard earned nest-egg, except a heap of black drenched ashes and a few broken hearts.

The morning broke gray and cheerless, as March mornings so often persist in doing, and the somber pall of mist which hung over bluff and prairie did little towards lifting the shadow that hung still heavier upon the hearts of Laban Hartland and his sorely tried family. Phyllis, however, possessed a spirit that neither weather nor calamity could dominate for long. There was a task to be performed, no matter how repellent to her woman's nature. This she had determined upon during the still watches of the night. She rose at the usual time, hoping by steady contemplation of the coming ordeal to reconcile herself to the inevitable, and though with a sore heart, she went about her ordinary duties with a smiling face.

The fire, she had learned from Joe Parilla, had gained some headway in her room before discovered by himself. The cash-box he had found rifled of its contents and upon the ground outside the window which was open.

"Burglary, theft and arson, Miss Phyllis," said he, "is a mixin' up of crime that would make hanging too good for the brute."

"Had he his suspicions? Well, he had no need to suspect, for he as good as knew. Had he not seen a man on a black horse gallop like mad down Linden Lane only ten minutes before he saw the flames? Jim Hereford's stallion was black."

"Hush, Joe," whispered Phyllis, "you're wrong? Don't repeat a word to a living soul that you have told me. There are other and worse men than Hereford who ride black horses." Then, she stooped and whispered in his ear. "Promise," she said, stepping back.

"You can trust me," he replied, and they separated. Shortly after breakfast Hartland and Parilla drove into Broncho City, with the understanding that Phyllis would overtake them on horseback. Their mission was to endeavor, on the strength of the disaster, to excite the sympathy of the bank managers that they would be induced to yield a financial point in their favor. Failing this, a secret understanding had been reached between Phyllis and her father, whereby they had mutually consented — and not without a terrible sacrifice of womanly pride on the part of the former — to address a joint appeal to Colonel Coboss for a week's delay. To their dismay, however, they found upon visiting the bank, that the President was out of town. In his absence, and manifestly to the "sincere regret" of the officials in charge, "it was impossible to extend to Mr. Hartland the accommodation sought."

As to Mr. Jonas Scrimp, whom they encountered on the bank steps, neither the news of the fire nor Hartland's desperate situation appeared to astonish or concern him in the least. "Lena had told him," so he said, "last evening of the burning of Miss Phyllis's apartments, and he was in consequence prepared to hear — though he offered no explanation of his assumption — that Mr. Hartland would not be able to meet the instalment. He regretted so much that his hands were tied, but his instructions from the Colonel were imperative."

It was now one. Two hours more and the bank would close. They crossed over to the Bull's Head, where they hoped to engage a messenger to carry the final appeal to Colonel Coboss. Laban, noticeably flurried and anxious, Phyllis, though her big violet eyes looked graver than usual and her manner a trifle more dignified than was her wont, had the same brave smile for the friends who pressed about her sympathetically. At the doorway of the hotel they almost walked into the arms of Jack Hardisty, whose face showed even more visible signs of concern than that of Laban Hartland.

"Our meeting is fortunate," he said, "I was on my way to place my time, my services and," he added in a lower tone for Hartland's ear only, "my bank account at your disposal."

"No! No! that cannot be," whispered Laban, "but perhaps." he said, raising his voice and turning to Phyllis, "Hardisty would consent to be our messenger."

"Are you mounted, Mr. Hardisty?" she asked.

"My horse cast a shoe," he answered, "I left him at the forge."

"My father has a letter for Colonel Coboss, a reply is imperative before three. Starlight will carry you. Your own saddle will fit her. Will you help us?"

Would he help them?

Five minutes later the big sorrel mare was galloping as fast as its stout heart and strong limbs would permit, and bearing Jack Hardisty along the steaming trail to Maverick Hall.

* * * * * * * *

It was a few minutes past two, and Hardisty had for the third or fourth time washed Starlight's mouth, and was in the act of cinching up the loosened girths preparatory for his crucial gallop, when Hereford appeared upon the gravel drive leading his black stallion fresh from the stable. At this same moment the master of Maverick with two letters in his hand stepped from out the French window of his study upon the piazza. Dismissing Hardisty with a curt bow from further service, he handed the two letters to Hereford and with the loud injunction that they were to be "delivered to Miss Hartland at the Bull's Head before three, and on no account to spare his animal," he re-entered the house.

At this same moment, Sarza, unperceived by Colonel Coboss, approached Hardisty. Placing a small packet in his hand, she enjoined him with terrible earnestness to "deliver it, no matter what the cost or hazard into Phyllis Hartland's own hands, prior to the letter given to Hereford by the Colonel." Then, she stayed an instant, long enough to see Jack Hardisty fling himself into the saddle and Starlight strike her stride in hot chase after the big stallion, already disappearing in the mist and mire, half a good mile away.

* * * * * * * *

Both men were past masters in the art of horsemanship. While Hardisty labored under the disadvantage of his own greater weight and a lighter animal, with a long gallop already to its credit, he soon discovered that the rougher shoeing of the mare enabled her to keep her footing on the stretches of yet frozen ground, and so cut the corners of the twisting trail that Hereford on his black stallion dare not try to negotiate. For the first mile or so he kept his mare well in hand, reserving her wind and endurance for the final three mile stretch of enclosed prairie road, towards which the barbed wire fences gradually converged and formed a pocket.

Hereford seemed to divine his rival's intention. The horse that could steal the lead at the entrance of the straight would probably hold it. The stallion responded to his appeal. The melted snow and black mud were thrown in showers from its heels, as it plunged along the vaporous trail. Outside, on the less yielding ground, the more regular thud of the mare's hoofs reached him. She was steadily gaining.

They were at last head to head, neck to neck, wither to wither. Black stallion and sorrel mare embossed with foam, their tightly drawn saddle girths audibly responding to their labored respirations.

No word was spoken. No whip was raised. Either would have been a waste of power. Each of the four knew the value of silent effort.

They were at the road's mouth now, and as they swung in from opposite sides narrowly escaped a collision. The moment for supreme action had come. With a sudden touch of the spur and simultaneous tightening of the reins, Hardisty fairly lifted Phyllis's mare to the front, the big black stallion was beaten, while Hereford's oath was

stifled by a snowball from Starlight's nimble heels.
On the home run, the sorrel, the lighter of the two,
though carrying extra weight, drew away from
the heavy stallion, now pretty well spent with its
previous pounding, and a few minutes before three,
covered with mud from head to foot, with the
mare almost hidden in a cloud of steam, Hardisty
was receiving sweet words of gratitude from
Phyllis Hartland, into whose hands he had surrendered the package in obedience to Sarza's
command.

It contained an amount in big gold coins sufficient to meet in full the instalment on Colonel
Coboss's mortgage, and was accepted with tears.

Hardly had this scene been enacted, when
Hereford, as dark as a thunder cloud, reined up his
spent stallion and presented to Phyllis a letter
marked " No. 1." It contained the following card

COLONEL REGINALD COBOSS,

Maverick Hall,
Broncho County, Iowa.

and a brief note which ran as under:

" If you will condescend to give me one word
of encouragement, write upon the enclosed card
' Yes,' over your own initials, and Hereford, who
is ignorant of the contents of either of these letters,
will hand to you the one marked ' No. 2 ' which

contains a receipt in full for all moneys and interest due me on the mortgage I hold upon your father's property."

For a moment a hot flush, not unnoticed by the three men, dyed Phyllis's noble face; then, in their presence she wrote upon Colonel Coboss's card a large and legible "No" and with a most gracious smile handed it to Hereford with a request that he would kindly give it to the master of Maverick "at his own convenience."

When five minutes later, Jonas Scrimp — who was in the bank only waiting for the clock to strike the hour of three in order to protest the defaulted note of Laban Hartland, with a view of serving through Dago Phil an immediate writ of ejectment — saw the portly form and smiling face of the laird of Cloverdale with his daughter on his arm, step up to the cashier's desk, you could have knocked him down with a butterfly's wing — but when he heard the chink and saw eagle after eagle of shining gold coin pushed through the brass railing and a certain promissory note handed over to Laban in return, he uttered an inarticulate cry and fled the building.

* * * * * * * *

That night the angel of peace spread her comforting wings over slumbering Cloverdale.

CHAPTER XVIII

A Jersey Beauty.

Though Sarza's timely generosity extricated Laban Hartland from what appeared at the moment irretrievable ruin, it was as a matter of fact merely a temporary reprieve. This he realized, and at times almost persuaded Phyllis into believing that it would have been better to have sacrificed his entire Cloverdale interest, for, he argued, was not Sarza's munificent gift an additional obligation and would not September inevitably bring with it the cast-iron obligations of another instalment?

But Phyllis, upon reflection, would not listen to so easy-going and seductive a contention. She declared she had yet to learn defeat. Much could be done in six months and she cast about with renewed activity for more profitable channels for her energies than seemed to lie within the capabilities of Spangled Hamburghs and music lessons, or Berkshire pigs and calisthenics.

About this time, the protracted spell of commercial depression and a sudden drop in the price of beef began to affect even the great cattle kings themselves, and Coboss, among others, found it more than convenient to send some of the choicest of his young stock to the " hammer."

The master of Maverick these days was by no means in the best of humors. His chagrin at the declination of his offer by Phyllis, and his resentment at being balked of his revenge, manifested itself among other ways in a suspicion as to Hereford's own feelings towards Phyllis, a suspicion not only reversed on Hereford's part and redirected towards the Colonel, but shared by the former with compound interest.

Colonel Coboss had anticipated a complete triumph over Phyllis Hartland's pride. Scrimp, with whom he was in constant communication, had informed him of her loss and he looked upon the fire as little short of a direct interposition of Providence on his own behalf. When, therefore, this realization of his hopes was negatived at the last moment by Sarza's ready succor — all unsuspected by him — he was led to believe that the explanation of Laban Hartland's escape from his dilemma was the result of some well concocted plan on the part of either Hereford or Hardisty. This view of things readily inspired a feeling of jealousy towards his own chief herdsman, and created the impression that that fellow Hardisty's respectful admiration for the " lass of Cloverdale " was not altogether distasteful to that young lady.

Meanwhile, the reverses of the last three years had not been void of profit even to Laban Hartland. Their influences, though felt, while hardly being admitted, were yet working a radical change in the hitherto set opinions of the perverse wheat king. This, Phyllis was not slow to discern, but had sufficient tact not to announce her discovery too hastily, for her apparent apathy only served to develop in her father a greater desire to put to practical proof the " articles " of his newly acquired faith.

"St. Lambert and I," he said to her one morning as with skirts and sleeves rolled up, she presented a most fetching appearance, as she busied herself regulating the milk pans in what she called her "buttery"—"have entered into a partnership, Phyllis."

"Oh! indeed, Daddy, I should have thought the Doctor's contemplated partnership with Ruth would have occupied all his attention."

"We have entered into an agreement," he went on somewhat astonished at her unusual indifference, "to cultivate a part of Cloverdale on shares. We have effected a compromise on crops. He is to plant corn and oats and clover, and I'm going to see how it is the Missouri Coteau can't raise sorghum and beet-roots and barley. I have been reading," he said, "a good deal of late"—and he flourished a ponderous volume entitled the "Sweetmeats of Trade"—"on the immense amount of undeveloped wealth there is in the cultivation of distillery products and I have fully decided that with a net profit of forty-five dollars per acre from sorghum alone, that—" but she did not wait for more, sidling up to him, she placed her cream white arms about his ruddy neck and kissed him.

"You are a great Daddy," she said. Then, with an arch look of studied indifference, "What's the matter with wheat?"

"Wheat!" he replied. "What's that you said? Wheat! Wheat! Why wheat—" then their eyes meeting they both laughed outright and she, releasing her hold of him, stepped into the middle of the floor and raising her skirts, com-

menced to piroutte about the room so rapidly that
he could see little but a vision of white petticoats
and gleaming ankles, while she danced on until
the milk pans upon the shelves jumped and slid
and jingled in unison, and kissed each other's
creamy lips because they could not help it.

Phyllis was not slow to recognize what her
father's divorce from wheat and matrimony with
mixed farming meant for Cloverdale and the future
prospects of the Hartland family. While Ruth's
future was happily assured and her own prospects
as regarded the matter of ways and means and her
own livelihood gave her little concern, there were
other vague dreams of a far different and more
personal future, in regard to which she felt, though
she hesitated to give the thought room, much less
expression, that Cloverdale and Cushla Range
would somehow or other be most intimately connected. This being so, it is little wonder that she
was more than delighted at her father's sudden
agricultural somersault, even if his new creed was
open to criticism. Was not St: Lambert taking
turn about at the horn of the plough, and was not
the transition from corn and clover to cows — with
a possible accent on the darling Jerseys — after all,
not such a remote possibility?

Now, all these facts and fancies greatly encouraged Phyllis Hartland, for ever since her
arrival at Cloverdale, and especially since Jack
Hardisty's notable speech at Broncho City town
hall, she was convinced that the only way that
Cloverdale would ever be freed from the incubus
of the mortgage, would be through the instrumentality of cows, and who knew but that these

"prong horned devils" were not destined to appear in the shape of Jersey beauties.

Subsequent events proved that Phyllis's intuition was only another name for clairvoyance.

March had gone out like a lamb and it was one of those pale, soft mornings in early April, when the biting storms and trying suspense of a long winter are forgotten in the advent of sunshine and renewal of hope, that Phyllis stood on the piazza at Cloverdale drinking in the ozone that drifted up from the twinkling prairie. She was deep in her own meditations. She was trying to solve to her own logical satisfaction the true inwardness of the motives that had induced Dago Phil to steal her money and set fire to Cloverdale. Of his guilt there was in her own mind now no shadow of doubt. His presence at the school house, the visit of the black horseman as described by Parilla, and yesterday the lace handkerchief exhibited to her by Lena, with the tearful admission that "Mr. Nigro had dropped it from his pocket" when he visited her the night of the fire all pointed to that conclusion. Lena's heart was torn, she sobbingly declared, at what she considered was proof positive of her lover's unfaithfulness. In this dainty bit of lace, Phyllis had recognized her own property, and well remembered having pinned it as an artistic bit of lingerie above her toilet table, before she rode to the school house.

The noise of steps upon the gravel drive to her right disturbed her. She raised her head. Coming towards her was a tall man, leading a young cow by a handsome halter. At the same moment, the noise of a shutting gate upon her left caused her to turn her head in that direction. Coming towards her from the Linden Lane was another tall man leading another young cow, by another hand-some halter.

She rubbed her eyes, and again shot a swift glance in either direction. The two groups were yet there, approaching but still preserving the same equi-distance. She rubbed her eyes again, but she could not efface the picture. Was it a mirage? At that moment a voice on the right said "So! Cushla" while a voice on the left said "Co! Bossy." That settled it. One minute later Jack Hardisty and Jim Hereford stood before her, each leading a cow!

The two men glared at each other. The two heifers lowered their heads and struck attitudes of defiance. For a few seconds there was the silence of the grave. Then Phyllis, glancing from one to the other, broke into a rich, infectious burst of laughter, in which both Hardisty and Hereford sorely against their inclinations were compelled to join.

"Forgive me," said Phyllis, controlling herself with difficulty, "but I am sure you gentlemen will admit that it is a funny coincidence. What can I do for you?"

"Permit me, Miss Hartland," said Hardisty, raising his hat and figuratively taking the bull by the horns, while he shortened his hold on the halter, "to present to you, if you will be pleased to accept it, a Jersey heifer known as "Merry Maiden," from the Cushla herd. May she be a credit to her new mistress and to her own breed."

"And allow me, Miss Hartland," said Hereford

bowing low and partly turning his back on Hardisty, "to ask your acceptance of a Shorthorn heifer, "Honeysuckle" by name, the pick of the Maverick ranch. Under your impartial management I have no fear but that the animal will sustain the unrivalled reputation of the breed. I would like to say though, that I had no idea that Mr. Hardisty contemplated waiting upon you this morning on a similar mission, or I should have timed my own visit accordingly."

"Nor had I any idea of Mr. Hereford's intentions," laughed Hardisty, "but had I known all about it, it would certainly not have interfered with my plans in the slightest."

Then Phyllis, while the heifers whisked their tails and regarded her wistfully with their soft brown eyes, thanked the two men with equal warmth, and assured them that no pains would be spared by her in educating the "darlings" as befitted their rank.

"I will treat the dear things with the most honest impartiality," she said, "and may the best cow win."

At the sales of stock which had recently been concluded by Colonel Coboss and Dr. St. Lambert, Hardisty and Hereford, inspired by the same feeling, but prompted by dissimilar motives, had, without the slightest suspicion of each other's intentions, secured the cows they had just presented to Phyllis.

They had also tried to allay the suspicions of their friends by almost identically the same line of argument.

At the moment that Hereford was assuring

Jonas Scrimp and Miss Tabitha that he "wanted to convince old man Hartland that Shorthorns paid better than wheat," Hardisty with unnecessary earnestness was explaining to Sarza that he "wanted to prove to the old gentleman that the Jersey cow was the sheet anchor of the farmer and the milky way to solvency."

On the following day, St. Lambert presented Phyllis with "Buttercup," the acknowledged queen of his selected Guernsey herd.

This quaint and triple presentation gave a singular impetus to the interest already manifested throughout the district in the several rival breeds. Though Phyllis's admitted preference was for the Jersey, Merry Maiden, she readily accepted the responsibility to extend to Honeysuckle and Buttercup equal opportunity to prove their superiority. The sincerity of this resolution no one challenged. Judge Phineas D. Quad, in an ensuing number of the Broncho City Rustler, editorially declared that "the country at large was more than willing that the question of bovine superiority should be determined by the competitive results attendant upon Miss Hartland's management, it being universally conceded that under that young lady's superintendence, the rights of each cow would be scrupulously conserved."

But there were those among the gossips who declared that Mrs. Quad had stated that the flamboyant diction of the Judge's editorial was inspired by a loftier motive than his mere passing interest in cows.

CHAPTER XIX

"The Milky Way."

It was not long before the extraordinary "trust" reposed in Phyllis Hartland, and the nature of her new enterprise, became not only the talk of the homestead, and the gossip of the town, and the ruling topic of conversation in the grazing districts of that section of the Missouri valley. The cowboys on the adjoining ranches gambled on the result. The farmers lingered too late for their own good in the market places, discussing the chances of their favorite breed and the success of Merry Maiden, Buttercup and Honeysuckle was recklessly pledged in milk shakes, cock-tails, lager and phosphates. Even the business men in the adjoining towns staked crisp bills of goodly denomination on the result, while jealous wives and their wondering daughters spilled many a bowl of rich cream, and dropped many a stitch, over the heated discussions which arose in dairy and kitchen.

It was not long, therefore, before Phyllis Hartland's dairy became the chief objective point of interest in the whole country side, not only for the residents of the county, but for commercial men and others who happened to sojourn for a night or so at Broncho City. The casual traveller became so impressed with the stories circulated in the rotunda of the Bull's Head, as to Miss Hartland's striking beauty, varied accomplishments and experimental dairy, that protecting himself behind the subterfuge of being an enthusiast in the matter of cows, he would hire a "rig" and drive out to Cloverdale in order to get a peep at Phyllis and her triplets.

Though disposed at first to offer but slight encouragement to this daily increasing display of cow curiosity, Phyllis, with her ready perception, soon devised an admirable way of converting the inquisitiveness of the visitors who flocked to worship at her shrine, to her own very material advantage. Under Jack Hardisty's superintendence, some modern but inexpensive stalls had been constructed, adjoining which was a small but complete buttery, reserved exclusively for the product of the three cows, with an office attached. In this, were systematically kept the daily records of each cow, showing quantities and value of food consumed, and amount and value of milk and butter. In the dairy the product of each cow was exhibited separately. Besides Ruth — who entered heart and soul into the scheme for the fun of the thing — Mrs. Dean was also pressed into service, so that some one or other of "the three handsome Misses Hartland" was always ready to introduce the visitors to the tiny, but exquisitely kept, barn and buttery.

It was, of course, pretty well understood that the product of the Cloverdale dairy was on the market. But if there was any doubt upon the subject, a visit to the buttery soon set the matter at rest.

Above the pats and rolls of appetizing butter

that shone like bunches of marsh mallows, were
cards denoting the price. Milk and buttermilk
were similarly advertised, and so it came to pass
that few visitors who " did " Cloverdale under the
guidance of Phyllis or her sisters, left without con-
tributing some silver tokens for samples of the
" milky way."

Indeed, from now on Phyllis encouraged pub-
licity for her experiments, and not only requested,
but insisted, that every visitor should critically inspect the methods of her treatment.   At each of
the two daily milkings, it was so arranged that
either St. Lambert, Hardisty or Hereford should
be present; these visits being so regulated as to
prevent, as far as possible the too frequent meeting of Hereford and Hardisty, between whom —
and it required no surgical operation to disclose
the fact — more than strained relations now existed.
Once every week, these three chiefly interested
spectators, however, would meet as a board of
reference and suggest any change of diet or treatment that they thought might be of benefit to the
particular animal in the success of which they
were specially concerned.

Among other very occasional visitors was Colonel Coboss of Maverick Hall. He avoided the
bungalow, however, as he would a rattlesnake.
Though his passion for Phyllis was rather inflamed
than dampened by her rebuffs, he was smarting
under the knowledge that he had not only made
an ass of himself generally, but had forfeited in
her eyes his claim to rank as a gentleman. As
his love lacked all nobility of purpose, which a
course of self criticism was not slow to reveal, it

is easy to understand that he became suspicious of every one, and regarded not only Hereford, but even Phyllis, as being capable of duplicity in order to attain their own ends.

Hence, and with a view of winning back his own prize — five hundred dollars meant a good deal to him these days — he had selected two choice young Shorthorn cows from his own herd to experiment with, the best of which he secretly intended at the last moment to enter for competition with Phyllis's trio at the State Fair.

At the back of all this was the unholy desire to break Laban Hartland, and bring Phyllis to her knees, and to make his action all the more regrettable and unlovely, he had admitted to his confidence, and enlisted as active recruits, Phil the Rustler and Jonas Scrimp. To the Hartlands, openly, he was all humility and sunshine.

The last days of August had introduced themselves with a blast of heat of sirocco-like intensity. Though the average temperature had not been quite as exalted as that of the previous summer, the drouth had again brought with it calamity and regrets. Laban's barley proved little more successful than had his wheat. His sorghum handicapped also by lack of expert cultivation, proved a failure, and his beet roots, though utilizable for stock purpose, were a dead loss as regarded sugar capabilities. St. Lambert's patch of oats had fared little better than Hartland's barley, though the corn, while below the average, was a passable crop.

It was the clover, however, that — anyway, in Phyllis's estimation, — redeemed all other disap-

pointments. The perfume of its pink and white
petals filled the valley, penetrated the cool halls of
the bungalow, and imparted an extra degree of
fragrance even to the breath of her cows, which
chewed its red tops and their own cud with
profitable persistence. A bunch of the sweet
flowers as long as they remained in bloom might
always have been seen resting on Phyllis's bosom,
while busy and adventurous bees bore its pollen
and its honey-dew even as far as Broncho City,
and rested their tired wings among the mignonette
at Crocus Cottage.

It was this suspected act of piracy on the part
of the bees that suggested to Miss Tabitha Scrimp,
who was nothing if not up to date — that is, if her
own estimate could be relied upon and partly
that she was governed perhaps by her own secret
feelings — to cease practising her favorite ballad,

"O! why hast thou taught me," etc.

She now extracted all the honey and comfort that
she could by the exercise of her own falsetto,
out of

"Where the bee sucks," etc.

This song she might have continued to harp
upon until the crack of doom, but that she
insisted with the spirit of curiosity inherent in her
sex—in order that she like any other true artist
might interpret the " ballade," as she termed it,
with proper feeling — upon visiting the home, as
Jonas cruelly expressed it, of the " suckers."

Her experience in this new field of exploration
is best described by herself.

" Would you believe it, my dear," said she to
Phyllis, " why, the horrid things seemed actually

to resent my appearance. See!" she continued hysterically, "they have stung me here and there and goodness knows where else, while my poor face—" and then she broke down, until Phyllis restored her equanimity by sympathetic words, and bathed her bitten limbs.

*　　　*　　　*　　　*　　　*

Chapter XX.

Love and Poison.

It was only a few days now before the opening of the State Fair, which was set for the 4th, 5th and 6th of September. The competition of the cows, however, was to cover a period of six days, which would extend the time of this special exhibit until the evening of the 9th. The judges of dairy stock, and the experts selected for passing judgment on the cows, comprising the special exhibit, according to the phraseology of the parti-colored posters, "the greatest and most unique test ever before attempted"—were dairymen of almost continental fame, and hailed from a distance. The decision of these men, wise in milk and butter, in solids and fats, was to be made known on the morning of the 10th, at about twelve o'clock.

When it is remembered that the tenth day of September was the fatal day upon which the semi-annual instalment on Colonel Coboss's mortgage would fall due, it can be understood what valiant energy and unsparing devotion Phyllis concentrated upon the members of her dairy, upon whose superior ability to chew the cud and assimilate the ensilage, all her hopes of Cloverdale now seemed to depend.

Through Sarza, she had also learned, to her amazement, of Colonel Coboss's secret "fitting out" of some of his own Shorthorns.

"Supposing," she said to Sarza, "that one of that bad man's own cows should take first prize!"

And the bare idea of so awful a possibility sent a cold shiver down their sensitive backs.

It was about this time that she extracted great comfort out of some words of Cornelius Kobb's, who in company with Mrs. Kobb — he was not permitted to visit without her escort — and several tow-headed off-shoots of the parent stem, had upon the last Sunday driven over to pay his first respects to Phyllis's hostages. Now, Cornelius was an acknowledged authority on "caows," and as Phyllis wanted to extract from him an uninterrupted expression of opinion, advantage was taken of the personal demands upon Mrs. Kobb by one of her unweaned offspring, to have a private view of Merry Maiden.

"You've got th' winner ol right, Miss Phlis," said Cornelius, as he ran his practised eyes over the animal and noted her prominent points. "Ther's yer long, slim, droopin' neck, and rale scrawny look a front of th' shoulder. Then thar's yer flat thighs. An' git on to th' great deep barrel of her, gal! Large enuf seein' she be wedge shaped, to store the hull o' th' silage in Cloverdale. An' see a' hyar," he exclaimed, as he hung his hat on one of her projecting hip bones, "thet takes th' cake, yu've got a caow, goldurn it, that puts her feed into milk, instead o' layin' it on all over'er back. She'll git thar, Miss Phlis, and don't yer fergit it!"

It had been agreed that St. Lambert, Hardisty and Hereford were each to undertake the respective responsibilities of transporting their own

especial protege to the fair grounds, and as this had
to be done in the cool of the day, they were invited
by Hartland to sleep at Cloverdale Sunday night.
Hereford, however, with expressions of regret, de-
clined. He had business in Broncho City. If they
would let him stable his splash-faced roan cayuse
— he never used his stallion for cattle work — he
would be out by cock crow in the morning.

This memorable Sunday evening was spent by
the Cloverdale household in the open air. Under
a variety of flimsy pretexts Laban was left by
himself to finish his cigar on the veranda, while
the others paired off, after offering the most in-
excusable excuses.

St. Lambert's was the only straightforward
and reasonable one; he " had a lot to talk about to
Ruthie." They disappeared in the shadows. Sarza
had promised Mr. Parilla to mend some Jersey
buttons for him in the kitchen, yet in the face of
this, they walked straight to the rustic bench under
the shadow of the windmill, and would probably
have been sitting there yet, if the pins and needles
in Joe's arm had not compelled him to shift his
position. Jack Hardisty pleaded so long with
Phyllis, that she finally consented to show him the
precise manner in which she attacked the fire a year
ago, but somehow or other, to this day, neither
of them can offer any explanation why they
deliberately turned their backs upon the pump-
house, and were lost to view in the bosky recesses
of the Linden Lane. But when they did appear
some two hours later, Phyllis's deep violet eyes
were shining with a more womanly and a holier
light, while her face reflecting the silver whiteness

of the pale moonbeams was radiant with an unutterable joy.

Let us for a while allow the shimmering sycamore leaves and Jack Hardisty's heart to remain
the sole repository of her secret.

* * * * * * * *

It was well on towards morning that St. Lambert, whose open bedroom window overlooked the
paddock, a hundred yards or more away, was
awakened by a sound of plunging and kicking in
the cow byres. Hastily arousing Hardisty, the
two men a moment later, half clad, were scudding
over the wet grass towards the stables. Upon unlocking the door, a strange and inexplainable sight
confronted them. Stretched upon the fresh straw
in Merry Maiden's stall lay Hereford's splash-faced
roan, groaning and writhing in agony. But where
was the cow? Rather, where were the cows? In
Buttercup's box alongside, Phyllis's big sorrel was
nibbling at some clover tops, and gave a neigh of
welcome, as the two men stared at each other in
speechless amazement. The next moment they
were more hopelessly dumbfounded, when on reaching Honeysuckle's stall, Hardisty's flea-bitten gray
recognized him with a whinny of surprise.

What did it all mean? Were they stark, staring mad, or — but at this moment in rushed Joe
Parilla and flew to Merry Maiden's manger.

"Doped!" he shouted. "Doped, Doctor!
doped as sure's there's a livin' hell for the knave
who did it." And he gathered together a few
handfuls of suspicious looking compound of mid-
dlings that had been finally rejected by Hereford's
pony. "But we're all right, Doc," he added,

" don't be scared, Merry Maiden's safe and so are
the others. Black Hereford's at last got a dose of
his own medicine."

" Black Hereford ! " they both exclaimed.

" Aye, Black Hereford," responded Joe. " It's
just this way," he continued, " suspectin' that there
might be some trickery afoot, last night with Miss
Phyllis's consent, I transferred — but what the
devil is this? " he cried suddenly, interrupting
himself, as he stooped and then held out a broad,
flat object at arm's length.

" Holy smoke ! " he shouted, as the moonlight
disclosed the identity of his find. " Phil Nigro's
hat, by th' eternal ! "

They administered a curative dose to the gray
gelding, and then strolled over to the stables to
satisfy · themselves as to the safety of the heifers,
while Joe Parilla concluded his story.

" It's just this way," he said, " ever since the
fire, I've been suspicious of the Coboss crowd,
knowing the ill will they bear the master, but —
and I'll admit I'm wrong — I have always in my
own mind blamed Hereford. This night's business, however, brings the crime home. Miss
Phyllis, God bless her! was right. Well, I exchanged the cows' quarters for the horses' stalls just
for the night. That's all there's to it. See," he said,
unlocking the stable door, where the three cows
lay quietly chewing their cuds, " they're all right.
But I took mighty good care," he added, " to put
Hereford's cayuse into Merry Maiden's place."

*   *   *   *   *   *   *   *

Meanwhile, Dago Phil was a fugitive from
justice.

Chapter XXI.

The County Fair and the Battle of Whips.

Broncho City, to use the language of Miss Tabitha Scrimp, which she borrowed from the columns of the Rustler, was "en fete." Banners, to quote from the same authority, flew from every point of vantage. Fortunately, no one was struck by these fugitive emblems of national pride and the most of them continued to float from pole and flag-staff during the entire week without extraordinary inconvenience to the citizens.

The dead walls of the prairie city were covered with flaming posters. In many of these, green calves were depicted wandering through blue pastures, pursued by vermilion shirted cowboys, while impossible yellow grooms fought with less possible pink stallions. These were supposed to rivet the attention of the country folk, and excite a wilder interest at the Fair Grounds — and they succeeded.

On other posters, white as snow, and well out of reach of the small boy and wanton vandal, were alternate paragraphs in blue and red letters, the announcement that one of the unrivalled attractions of the Fair would be the great six days special competition between the three selected Jersey, Guernsey and Shorthorn cows, the property of Miss Phyllis Hartland of Cloverdale against them-

selves and all other animals that might be entered
in an original and unique " Butter Test."

This, it went on to say, was for the purpose of
deciding for all time, as far as Iowa was
concerned, the moot question as to which breed
was to be recognized as (and this was in enormous
capitals)

"THE MORTGAGE LIFTER OF THE FUTURE!"

Here followed a list of prizes, the first, of
course, being that of Colonel Coboss, which was
referred to as

"THE MUNIFICENT DONATION
of
Five Hundred Dollars, Presented by the Master of
Maverick Hall; also that of
Two Hundred and Fifty Dollars, Presented by Dr. St.
Lambert of the Cushla Ranch; and that of
Fifty Dollars, Presented by James Hereford, Esq.
With One Hundred Dollars Additional, Presented by
the Broncho County Live Stock Improvement
Association."

The whole of which was to go, free of all impost
or entrance fee, to the animal accorded the greatest
number of points by the special committee of
expert judges selected for the purpose.

As Colonel Coboss rode by and read these for
the first time, he lowered his head over the pommel
of his saddle and cursed the judges whom he knew
to be honest, cursed Dago Phil, cursed the wide
world and everyone in it, and wound up by
cursing himself.

When Phyllis Hartland drove by with her
father and read the portentous poster for the first

time, she looked skywards, offered a silent appeal, thanked God for the mere pleasure of existence, and the possession of a Jersey cow, and had a splendid smile and a charitable thought for every one.

A few minutes before the hour for receiving entries expired, Coboss requested the acceptance by the judges of two Shorthorn cows, Cowslip and Wild Rose of similar age to those already listed, which he had been requested, he explained, at the last moment to enter for competition. The committee for the reception of stock, having no other alternative, received the entries.

The weather was of the same delicious brand as that described by Father Hennepin in his own florid way, and which he experienced when he ascended the Mississippi over two centuries before. It was typical (in the language of the Iowa Indians) of Iowa the "Beautiful Land;" the land of those who had long since surrendered their unassessed acres to cruel Sioux and crafty Osage, and were driven across the mighty Missouri into the remoter west. Hence everyone was in holiday attire, the war paint and feathers of civilization.

The "three handsome Misses Hartland," to wit, Dorothy (Mrs. Dean), Ruth and Phyllis, were all costumed alike, and, to quote the colloquialism of the members of the Broncho City Business Men's Association, were "simply immense." They were gowned in dresses of pale gray summer cloth with artistic touches of white here and there, and white sailor hats adorned with artificial clusters of Phyllis's beloved purple and white clover, natural bouquets of which, fresh

from the meadow, they also wore upon their
bosoms.

Everyone was on the tiptoe of expectation, and
when the park gates were finally thrown open at
ten o'clock, the crowds of "vaccinated" humanity
as St. Lambert called them, surged into the
grounds.

The dairy tests were conducted in a building
especially set apart for the purpose, to which no
one was admitted without a pass, other than those
in attendance upon the competing cows, the feed
of which was zealously guarded under lock and
key. Twice, however, during the day the five
now famous creatures would be led around the
show ring by silk halters, in the hands of stalwart
herdsmen, and to the fanfare of bugles and music
of a brass band, and other harmless devices, calculated to whet the appetites of rural visitors. In
addition to the local cattle talent there were
breeders and buyers from not only neighboring
but distant states, for Broncho County Fair had an
established reputation in all stock centers, and
many a good hoof and horn picked up "on the
side" repaid the eastern buyer for his long journey.

As for diversions, they were innumerable.
The bearded lady, the petrified man, the snake
charmer, the only and original wizard of the wild
and wooly west, the juggler, the contortionist,
and the abbreviated skirt dancer, all under one
canvas — and it might be as well to add, all
represented by the same versatile young man —
did a roaring trade. And when the cool shades of
evening descended upon this innocent and bucolic
center and reputedly ragged edge of civilization,

then the chorister-faced cowboy and saintly broncho-buster would conduct the "petrified man" from the east into some quiet joint, and there introduce him to prairie cock-tails, and the costly mysteries of "freeze-out."

Good, simple minded Miss Scrimp was also there—not in company with the petrified man, of course,—having stacks of fun in her own quiet way among the needle and art work, the vegetables and flowers, the dairy exhibit and the side-shows, with Sarza or the Cloverdale trio.

"Flitting," as she expressed it to Hereford, "like a busy bee, you know, extracting all the honey I can, but"—as he turned to leave her—"never stinging a soul!" And she gurgled and giggled at the humor of her speech, blind to the truth of her own honest utterance.

Lena was also there in company with Roxie, wearing her heart away for faithless Dago Phil. whose absence greatly perplexed her, and marvelling what made Jonas Scrimp so irritable when she asked if "he'd seen Mr. Nigro." Daisy Dean was of course there with wide open eyes, drinking in everything and wondering what would happen to little girls like herself, if they "chewed gum" as persistently as Aunt Phyllis's cows chewed their cuds.

As for Laban Hartland, ropes could not have held him back. His pride in his daughter and his duty as a representative granger had overcome his scruples, and for the time at least, his deeply rooted dislike to the "prong horned devils" was relegated to the background.

But even county fairs and competitive dairy

tests must come to an end. Phyllis, who throughout the trying contest had longed for the hour of
the final milking, now looked forward to the
morrow with her senses wrought to the highest
tension, for upon the results of the test it seemed
to her, at times, as if not only her own life and the
future of Cloverdale and all its inmates, but the
prosperity of all of Broncho County equally
depended.

As to the feeding of her own cows, the food
had been weighed and served to them according to
the fancy of Hardisty, Hereford and Dr. St.
Lambert under her own supervision, however,
and subject to the inspection of the committee who
kept a record of the amount and value of the food
eaten. The bill of fare thus provided was a liberal
one and did not lack for variety. Hay, silage,
bran, cornhearts, a snack of oil meal once in a
while, with a carrot now and then for dessert.
As far as Phyllis could gather from the partial
information vouchsafed to her by the judges, the
order of merit among her own triplets was as
follows, Merry Maiden, Buttercup and Honeysuckle. But the actual amount of milk and butter
produced was not the only thing to be considered.
There was the quality, and the value and the
net profit all to be taken into account, after
deducting the cost of feed.

There were also the physical points of each
cow to be criticized and passed upon.

As to Colonel Coboss's two cows, she could
obtain no information whatever, but as "dark
horses," she felt they were her most formidable
competitors.

" Heigh ho!" sighed poor Phyllis, as she laid
her weary head upon her pillow after Friday's
tremendous tax upon her energies. " Heigh ho!
last year a fire and now a dairy test for the
heaviest stakes ever competed for,—a woman's
happiness! I wonder what it will be next year."
Then like a flash a certain possibility dawned
upon her. With cheeks aglow she checked the
temptation for further reflection and in another
moment was sleeping as peacefully as a child.

*   *   *   *   *

" Having completed our statements compiled
from the registers as kept and verified by us, I
have much pleasure, Mr. President, Ladies and
Gentlemen, in announcing our unanimous verdict
in regard to the order of merit of the five cows
which have for the last five days been competing
in the most unique and exciting contest that it has
ever been our privilege to witness."

Thus spake Mr. Bronson Sibley, the famous
dairying expert and chairman of the special committee.

It was twelve o'clock, noon, of Saturday, the
10th of September, and the stock ring in the driving
park was massed with people collected to hear the
decision of the judges. Everyone interested was
present. The chief participators — exclusive of
the cows themselves — were positively pale with
the long strain and suppressed excitement. Phyllis
Hartland's face was like a piece of white marble,
its quality intensified by the depth of her glorious
violet eyes.

" We find," continued the speaker, and the
silence of the crowd was painful, " we find that,"

and here he re-adjusted his glasses, while Hardisty surreptitiously patted Phyllis's hand, "we find that the order of merit is as follows,—First, the Jersey, Merry Maiden, Miss Phyllis Hartland, owner." He got no further. If all the Sioux and Osages and Iowas, who had ever camped on the banks of the Missouri had united in one compound warhoop, it would have been as a hiccough compared to the roar which now arose from the lungs of the Broncho County citizens.

A mist arose before Phyllis's eyes, and genuine tears of thankfulness gemmed their lids. "God was so good, and Cloverdale was safe." Mr. Bronson Sibley was again speaking.

"Taking 100 points as the standard of perfect excellence, we find that the cows rank as follows: Merry Maiden 85; Buttercup 74; Honeysuckle 72; Cowslip 71; Wild Rose 68. He had now very great pleasure in handing Miss Phyllis Hartland four separate checks, amounting in all to nine hundred dollars, the sum of the four joint prizes, all secured by the superlative excellence of her magnificent Jersey, Merry Maiden, and her own faithful management."

*　　*　　*　　*　　*　　*　　*　　*

As the clock was on the stroke of one, that same afternoon, Laban Hartland, accompanied by Phyllis, deposited to the credit of Colonel Coboss the Colonel's own cheque for five hundred dollars made payable to the winner of the first prize in the special dairy competition, and now by Phyllis's endorsement made re-payable to the maker, her father receiving in exchange therefor and through the same brass railing as in March last, his own notes given as security for the instalment due on the Cloverdale mortgage for the same amount and now lifted!

On this occasion Jonas Scrimp took very excellent care not to be a witness a second time to his own humiliation.

CHAPTER XXII

A Proposal, A Refusal, and the Battle of Whips.

Phyllis Hartland's victory was complete and the cup of her contentment was overflowing. As for Jersey cows in general and Merry Maiden in particular, words failed her when she essayed to express her admiration and gratitude. She had not only been able, through Jack Hardisty's wise and thoughtful present, to pay off another of the dreadful instalments on that awful mortgage, but she had returned to Sarza half of the loan so generously advanced last March. She had also been able out of the profits arising from the sales of eggs and poultry and a few nice young pigs and the "temporary renting," as she called it, of her "manners" and her "voice," to deposit a substantial sum in the savings bank.

If Phyllis's sudden ascent into enviable notoriety, and her extraordinary successes, had astonished her father, the climax to his amazement was reached when he discovered that she had also deposited to the credit of his own bank account the sum of two hundred dollars.

"Daddy dear," she said when he tenderly upbraided her, "I thought perhaps you were longing to experiment with some new kind of seed wheat, so —" but he stopped her mouth with kisses.

"Don't talk to me about wheat," he said, "wheat's not in it with Jerseys. Why, you can buy American wheat in England for sixty cents a bushel, while two pounds of Jersey butter are worth more than that in Broncho City, besides which, with Merry Maiden's help, you can 'grow' that amount of butter in one day."

The following morning much to her bewilderment, she found a strange Jersey cow from the Cushla ranch in the spare stall adjoining Merry Maiden's. Tied to the halter was this note —

"Dear Phyllis : — Please accept this 'prong horned devil' from your loving father, who has named it 'Mascot' in evidence of the faith that is in him."

But among Phyllis's roses there were some aggressive thorns. Hereford's daily attendance on Honeysuckle during the days of preparation and competition had thrown him more closely into the society of Hartland's family than he had ever dared to hope. Blind to everything but his own mad infatuation for Phyllis, he misconstrued her many little acts of attention — which were the mere expressions of an impulsive and womanly sympathy for his empty life — into evidences of her regard.

"Give me," he said, seizing her hand one day almost roughly, and speaking in hurried, hoarse tones, "some open token of your regard, Phyllis. God alone knows how I love you!"

"Hush!" she replied, knowing that her heart was beyond the reach of such as him, yet sorry to shatter his dream. "That can never be."

Then a demon possessing him, he railed against Hardisty, and in his jealous fury taunted her with

the value of his own present, and left her with the
cowardly imputation that connivance and neglect
were alone responsible for Buttercup's defeat.

As a proper sequel to this, Joe Parilla drove
Buttercup over to Maverick Hall the following
morning with a note from Phyllis to Jim Hereford,
returning his present with "painful regrets" and
suggesting that "under his own management, a
victory over Merry Maiden would of course be
assured when they next met in competition." A
statement showing the cow's net profit while in
Phyllis's keeping was also enclosed together with
a check for the full amount thereof, and drawn
upon her savings bank account.

Hereford had not long to wait for the opportunity he desired. The State Fair occurred during
the last days of September, when a wider field of
competition was presented to the Broncho County
breeders. The contest, however, which was only
one of "points," resulted in a sweeping victory
for Phyllis's stable, Merry Maiden capturing the
first prize easily and winning "hands down," as
Laban Hartland subsequently imparted to Miss
Scrimp, and much to that simple minded lady's
bewilderment.

The outcome of this second competition made
the master of Maverick furious. Not only had he
his trouble for nothing, but he regarded this latter
defeat in the light of a public disgrace. "The
good name of Coboss, by gad! was being trailed
in the dust." Added to all of which he dropped
another five hundred dollars in the shape of a side
bet with Dr. St. Lambert.

If Hereford had been wild before, he was now

raging. Driven desperate by Phyllis's refusal and the banter of the cowboys at the return of his present, he sought an early opportunity to take his revenge out of no less a personage than Jack Hardisty. His charges and their threats were not long in reaching the ears of the man for whom they were intended, who promptly sought out his traducer. The annual "round up" was in progress on the Maverick range, and when Hardisty rode into camp, he found a big mob of cowboys engaged in "cutting out" and "branding" under Hereford's direction. Riding up to the latter in the presence of the crowd who were anticipating trouble, he demanded of Hereford that he should withdraw or substantiate his charges. Black Jim's only reply to this was to reiterate them.

"Then you are both liar and scoundrel," said Hardisty, riding towards him, "and must be made to eat your words."

"And pray who will make me?" asked Hereford.

"I," answered Hardisty rising in his stirrups as he unwound his stock whip and brought the circling lash with a crack like a rifle across the other's shoulders. "Drop that toy," he cried, as Hereford reached for his revolver, "take your medicine like a man."

Then ensued a rare exhibition of stock whip skill and horsemanship. They rode at and around and upon and even on each other, exchanging and parrying the cruel sting of the black whirling whips as best they might. The air sung with the angry swish and pistol-like report of the heavily loaded lashes, and the snorts of the suffering ponies who resented their share of involuntary punishment.

Watching his chance, Hardisty at last swung his long lash so that it coiled like a lariat round his opponent's neck and with a mighty jerk on his whip-stock unhorsed and well-nigh strangled him. Then he dismounted merely to satisfy himself that the punishment he had inflicted was not of a serious nature, and excusing himself to the admiring crowd he rode away.

Jim Hereford's public humiliation was cruelly complete.

CHAPTER XXIII

Merry Maiden Wins the Blue Ribbon.

The snows of winter had descended upon Cloverdale once more. The summer song of the purling Osage river was silenced and o'er bluff and plain, valley and highland, a mantle of glistening crystal spread its protecting folds.

The same harmless rounds of pleasure had been indulged in as those of the previous winter, but the perpetual motion of the wheels of fate had so far evolved nothing of sufficient importance to disturb the even tenor of the Hartlands' ways. At the beginning of the new year, however, an incident occurred which was destined to lead to a revolution in the fortunes of the Massachusetts exiles, such as Laban even in his wildest wheat dreams only had dared to conceive.

It was a stormy night. A blizzard was rioting among the complaining branches of the leafless sycamores and piling up white dunes and drifts of snow across the piazza of the bungalow, when Roxie opening the hall door in response to a peremptory ring, let in a shower of frosty particles and a tall stranger.

Hartland himself was deep in the pages of a quarto volume on the "Dehorning of Cattle," Ruth was inditing an extraordinarily long letter to St. Lambert, who was absent in the east, while Phyllis was knitting her fair forehead over a trial balance sheet of eggs and bacon, butter and cheese. Upon the card which Roxie handed her master was engraved

****
*   *
*   *
*   *
*   MR.. E. F. VALANCEY,   *
*   *
*   *
*   American Jersey Cattle Club, New York. *
****

"Yes," said the tall, fine looking man, in answer to Hartland's query, "I have a big contract on hand. In the interests of the Cattle Club I represent I am scouring the country in order to secure the best twenty-five Jersey cows obtainable to compete in the World's Columbian Exposition Dairy Tests next May. I understand that Miss Phyllis Hartland has at least one very remarkable cow. I have travelled a great many hundred miles to see that cow. Can I see her?"

"Most assuredly," said Hartland, "he could on the morrow. O, no! he must not dream of returning to the city. Cloverdale always had a spare room for the belated traveller. My daughters, Mr. Valancey, Miss Phyllis, Miss Ruth."

In ten minutes they were old friends, and before they wished the tall man good night, they had learned more hard practical truths about dairy matters and Jersey cows than they had hitherto dreamed of.

A critical examination of Merry Maiden the following morning resulted in her selection as a competitor in the projected dairy tests, the greatest

the world had ever heard of, or is likely to hear of
again. Then, the tall expert, who Phyllis declared
was "one of the most entertaining men she had ever
met," bade them goodbye. "He had an appointment," he said, "with a cow in Southern Texas the
day after tomorrow. Business and the consideration due to the sex would not allow him to keep
her waiting."

* * * * * * * *

The tenth day of March had come and gone.
The instalment on the mortgage, thanks to Merry
Maiden's successes at the State Fair and the dairy
efforts of Buttercup, Mascot and herself had been
duly met. Colonel Coboss, upon whose prejudiced
Shorthorn mind the light was at last beginning to
break, had offered Phyllis five hundred dollars for
Merry Maiden, only to be refused. Nettled at
this, he made a bet in a moment of pique and
against his better judgment, of one thousand dollars with St. Lambert, that the Shorthorn selected
from his own herd for the Columbian Test would
beat Merry Maiden's individual record when they
met there in competition.

When May came, and, under the direction of
expert Mr. Valancey, Merry Maiden was trans-
ported to her quarters in the Jersey barns at
Jackson Park, Chicago, the eyes of every man,
woman and child in Broncho County, and in some
instances their steps, were turned in the direction
of that vast western metropolis.

Among these latter were Phyllis and Ruth
Hartland, Sarza and Miss Scrimp, who were
piloted by Dr. St. Lambert, and finally took up
their abode for the ensuing summer under the

sheltering roof of an old eastern friend. Mrs.
Dorothy Dean remained behind to direct the interior economy of Cloverdale, it being understood that Laban and Joe Parilla would also
remain to care for farm and stock until the middle
of September, when there would be a grand re-
union of all the Broncho County notables within
the inviting walls of the great White City.

  * * * * * * * *

The summer had passed and gone. May, June,
July and August had flown by to Phyllis and her
party as if on rainbow wings, so saturated and en-
tranced had they been with the glory and the
glamour of the complex scene. And now September had arrived, and with its mellow splendor had
softened the outlines of the white palaces, and
spread a veil, as it were of pale gossamer, over
the intense blue waters of restless Lake Michigan.

During these many weeks, which seemed to
her with their artistic recitatives of blue and gold,
crimson and purple, more like the pages of an il-
luminated ancient missal than a tangible, audible
and visible "fair," she succeeded in exhausting
herself in her unsuccessful efforts to exhaust the
programme.

Cornelius Kobb even, who about this time arrived upon the scene, and who several times had
tried to spring a local cattle-judge's badge upon a
Jackson Park gate-keeper, had finally to admit that
Broncho County "was not in it."

But when tired of all else, Phyllis always found
rest for mind and body at the Jersey Barns, a
"pass" to which had kindly been presented to her
by busy Mr. Valancey, from whom, as well as

from Merry Maiden, she always received an effusive welcome and a refreshing draught of her beloved Jersey milk.

The dying days of the month brought Laban Hartland and Joe Parilla, accompanied by Jack Hardisty, who knew almost as much about Chicago as he did about the coteau of the Missouri.

The success of the Jersey Herd, largely owing to the untiring vigilance of the "tall expert" was expected to be phenomenal, and the indications were that Jersey breeders were not to be disappointed. Among the more prominent of many stock men and exhibitors present was Mr. C. I. Hood of Lowell, Massachusetts, which latter fact alone, independent of his being one of the greatest breeders of Jerseys in the land and an authority on dairy stock, naturally drew Phyllis to him, especially so when he displayed a consuming business interest in the success of Merry Maiden.

The momentous day was close at hand now. Tomorrow, the 27th of September, was to witness the conclusion of the third of this unparalleled series of dairy competitions in all three of which Merry Maiden had been a conscientious cud chewer. Excitement ran so high the night preceding, that Laban suggested the "Midway" as an alterative, and they visited the Ostrich farm at his request. He had an idea that there would be money in ostriches at Cloverdale — he had a pamphlet on the subject — and rather resented Hardisty's advice that he had better take one to the hotel "some other evening." Phyllis pleaded for Hagenbach's circus, Ruth entreated for the Ferris Wheel, and naughty Miss Scrimp for the Persian theatre. All their wishes if not their tastes were duly gratified.

*   *   *   *   *   *   *   *

The auspicious day and hour, pregnant with such wonderful possibilities for the Hartland family, had arrived, and been inscribed on the records of time, and the triumph of the Jersey Herd as a whole, of Merry Maiden as an individual cow, and of Phyllis Hartland, was beyond all expectations absolute and complete.

The results can best be described in Phyllis's own words, who in a letter addressed to the editor of the Broncho County Rustler for publication, wrote in part as follows: —

"Dear Sir: — Merry Maiden competed in all of the three tests, in each of which tests a similar number of selected cows, Shorthorns, Guernseys and Jerseys were entered. No. 1 was a test for cheese and by-products, in which twenty-five animals of each breed competed. It occupied fifteen days from May 12th to 26th. . No. 2 was the ninety-day test, and lasted from May 31st to Aug. 28th. Just think of it! No wonder that my poor Merry Maiden got a little tired. She was not really herself for six weeks, quite under the weather, on one occasion she dropped in two days from yielding thirty-six pounds of milk to thirteen pounds, and at that time she was *leading* all the other seventy-four cows in butter. She finished second in this test, though, notwithstanding. No. 3 was the butter test from August 29th to September 27th, and lasted thirty days. In this contest only fifteen animals of each breed competed.

Now as to the result, and this will set at rest for all time the no longer moot question of superiority, and make another meeting in Broncho City town hall quite unnecessary, for it both shows the collective superiority of the Jerseys as a breed and also as individual cows. In the front rank of all stands Merry Maiden. In the Grand Sweepstakes Awards the following is the official decision of the Testing Committee selected by Mr. Buchanan, who is Chief, you know, of the Department of Agriculture of the World's Fair:

For the best *individual* cow in *each* breed competing. Merry Maiden.

For the best *individual* cow in *any* breed competing, Merry Maiden.

For the best *five* cows in *each* breed competing, Jerseys.

For the best *five* cows in *any* breed competing, Jerseys.

For the *best breed* competing, Jerseys.

The Guernseys came second and the Shorthorns last.

You will perhaps be surprised when I tell you that the cost of conducting these wonderful tests was $125,000. This is what was proved, however: my beloved Jerseys gave more milk; made more cheese; made more butter; gave more solids other than butter fat; required less milk to make a pound of cheese or a pound of butter; produced a pound of butter at less cost; made both cheese and butter of a higher quality and also proved that they were able to assimilate — I believe that is the correct word — a greater quantity of feed, and return a greater increased net profit than either the Guernseys or the Shorthorns.

The above are the perhaps not romantic, but very material facts, which I present to you as a text upon which you can build some of your clever editorial sermons for the benefit of our dairy loving friends.

Yours faithfully,

PHYLLIS HARTLAND.

*   *   *   *   *   *   *   *

CHAPTER XXIV

Merry Maiden Lifts the Mortgage and Brings Wealth and Wedlock.

Letter from Phyllis Hardisty to Laban Hartland.

"Deer Jump," Lowell, Mass.,
October — 1893.

Dear, dear Daddy: —

Here we are at last, thanks to Mr. Hood's kind invitation, which I need hardly say we do not regret having accepted. My conscience smites me for not having written to you sooner, but as you say the telegrams reached you all right, I honestly believe that it was just as well I didn't for Jack is perpetually at my elbow, and I am afraid my writing would have been illegible.

Yes, indeed! daddy dear, we have much to be thankful for. Merry Maiden has literally been our mascot and sheet anchor. What with prize money, purchase money, and profit on her product, the mortgage on Cloverdale is lifted at last. And O, what a nightmare it has been! The fire, dear old Jack's race with poor Jim Hereford, and the money from Sarza, are they not indelibly impressed on my memory! (Dear, kind Sarza!) So she is Mrs. Parilla at last? (Sarza Parilla) It's too ridiculous, and yet what a world of relevance there is in it all. The influence of "Sarsaparilla" has really entered into our very lives, for I suppose if it had not been

for the fortune made out of Hood's Sarsaparilla,
Mr. Hood would never perhaps have purchased
Merry Maiden, and the "Romance of Merry
Maiden " — of which I am mailing you a copy —
would never have been written.

So Jonas Scrimp has left Broncho City and
moved to the far west? I am not surprised, only
sorry for poor Tabitha. However, she must come
and stay with us. I am not a bit revengeful,
daddy dear, but it only seems right that Dago Phil
should be punished to the full extent of the law.
You say he is awaiting his trial? Is it really imperative that I should be a witness? Jack tells me
that Mr. Hereford has sailed for Mashonaland,
South Africa, you know. Ah me! it's a queer
world, isn't it dad? Do you know that you are a
dear old daddy? Not many persons would have
treated Colonel Coboss as you have done, after all
his persecution. Did you really take a mortgage on
Maverick Hall and are you going to insist on
"immediate ejectment, by gad, sir!" unless the
instalments are promptly paid up? I pray and
fully believe he will come out of it all a better
man. The whirligig of time brings about strange
things, doesn't it?

I had a long letter, if you please, from Ruth.
It was written from Paris. They are evidently
having a great time. She enclosed a scrap from a
society paper, in which it spoke of Dr. and Mrs.
Maryann St. Lambert of Iowa as staying at the
Hotel Americaine. Well, we are staying *here,* and
thankful I am for it too. The place is too delicious
for anything, and if it wasn't for Jack, I think I
should envy Merry Maiden her future lot.

"Deer Jump" is not in Lowell. You have to pass through Belvidere suburb to reach it, and through long stretches of softly rolling meadow-lands, fields of ripe grain, and orchards with bending branches of riper fruit. The buildings of the great Hood stock farm can be seen from a distance of miles. The final approach to the farm is extraordinarily impressive, sweller than Cloverdale, daddy. The entrance is through two massive stone gateways that invite you to enter in a reliable and protective sort of way. On the left, a beautifully kept carriage-road sweeps past the manager's handsome residence and on to the big imposing barns, where among fifty or more superlatively beautiful Jerseys, Merry Maiden now stands the queen!

The barns and the way the business is conducted is a revelation to Jack and myself, and we spend most of our time inspecting. The way they handle the ensilage would interest you immensely. Jack says his, as he thought, *original* idea of storing fodder like the Egyptians and sealing it hermetically for future use, is here in actual course of progress. As fast as the corn is brought from the field it is fed to the ensilage cutter on the second floor, which, after cutting the stalks, leaves and cobs all into uniform sized pieces, nearly an inch long, dumps them into the six immense silos, each of which holds a hundred tons. It took one hundred and fifteen loads to fill one of these pits. Just fancy! When they are packed down as closely as possible, they are made practically air-tight. We must have one on a small scale at Cloverdale, daddy. Goodness knows we have lots of room.

Some hundred yards or so beyond the barns is Mr. Hood's summer residence, such a charming place with long, wide verandas from which you can obtain as picturesque vistas as one could hope to find in all America; but then, you see it's in Massachusetts!

Through the intervening fields of verdure and grain which encompass the house, the Merrimack river winds its interrupted course, full of the chatter and music of "riffle" and rapid. Tradition, too, is not idle here, for an old Indian legend lends additional romance to the nomenclature of "Deer Jump." Set all this, daddy near, in a frame of soft blue mountains that lovingly girdle the place and you will have a very fair idea of the wonderful Hood Farm.

Jack says that I have not told you that Mr. Hood has not only secured Merry Maiden, but that he prides himself upon possessing her dam, her grandam, daughter, granddaughter and grandson. Six generations! He knows a good thing when he sees it, dad. He has promised me a calf from the "famous strain" the first opportunity. I have told him he should call Merry Maiden's stock, the "Mortgage Lifting Brand."

* * * * * * * *

Jack and I have just been wondering, daddy, dear, if you lived in the same kind of paradise when you were married, as we do. But why ask? Of course, no two people were *ever* as happy as we are!

Your proud, happy and devoted daughter,
PHYLLIS HARDISTY.

* * * * * * * *

P. S.   What's the matter with wheat and how about " prong horned devils? "

*   *   *   *   *   *   *   *

"May God bless her! " said Laban, " a noble daughter makes a good wife," and kissing Phyllis's letter tenderly he reverently placed it in his swelling bosom.

*   *   *   *   *   *   *   *

Laban Hartland is now one of the most enthusiastic stockmen in the west.   His meadows, however, are sacred to Jerseys to the exclusion of all other kine, where udder deep in fragrant red clover and sweet upland hay his fawn colored " mascots " cease not to chew the profitable cud, which brings contentment to themselves and prosperity to their owner.